Bed Rest

Bed Rest

Sarah Bilston

HarperLargePrint
An Imprint of HarperCollins*Publishers*
www.harpercollins.com

Excerpt from "This Be the Verse" from *Collected Poems* by Philip Larkin. Copyright © 1988, 2003 by the Estate of Philip Larkin. Reprinted by permission of Farrar, Straus, and Giroux, LLC.

HarperLargePrint
An Imprint of HarperCollins Publishers
10 East 53rd Street
New York, NY 10022.

ISBN: 0-06-112068-5

Printed in the U.S.A.

10 9 8 7 6 5 4 3 2 1

For Daniel and Maisie

acknowledgments

Thanks to Daniel Markovits and Sharon Volck-hausen, who provided incredibly helpful suggestions and advice on law firm life and landlord-tenant law. Daniel read and commented on about seventeen drafts of this novel, encouraged me to write it in the first place, and (as always) sustained me throughout. My mother, Barbara, has also helped me more than I can say.

In addition I want to thank my agents, Kathy Anderson at Anderson Grinberg and Kevin Conroy Scott at Conville and Walsh, for their superb guidance over the past few years. I'm indebted to Benjamin Markovits for his thoughtful and practical advice on writing and publishing, and to Sheila Fisher and my colleagues at Trinity College for generously granting me leave to work on the book and for providing such a happy and stimulating work environment.

Finally, I want to thank Alison Callahan, Jeanette Perez, and everyone at HarperCollins for their wonderful editorial guidance and warm, unstinting support.

1

I haven't written a diary since I was twelve. Wait, that's not true. I kept one for about six months when I started dating Mike Novak. I still have the notebook somewhere, a scruffy green ring-binder half filled with teenage angst about Mike and his terrible kissing and his lamentable desire for a student nurse named Susie.

Writing a diary seems like an admission you have nothing better to do. It's the life story of a person who doesn't have a life. And frankly, I'm not sure that anybody's existence is worth recording for posterity, unless you're a world leader or a Theatrical Great or something. Maybe not even then. I read my grandmother's diary once, it was all about the weather and her trips to the Women's Institute and the progress of her runner beans. I'd rather leave no record of my existence than that. I'd rather my life was a big blank page, so my future granddaughter can imagine me as a toothsome lovely whose youth was one long succession of olive-skinned, silk-shirted men.

On the other hand, when you really **don't** have anything better to do, writing a diary is as good a way of passing the time as any other. It makes the hours and minutes seem less of a vacuum—

I thought, I felt. I existed. I suppose I'll just have to hide this book from any future grand-daughters.

This afternoon, I left my office early, just before three. I work at—wait, why am I telling myself this? I know where I work.

Time for the first admission. I'm an anxious obsessive. I hate gaps and omissions; I have to record **everything**. That green ringbinder started out normally enough ("Mike Novak has a tanned chest and nipples that flush brown when I pull them with my teeth") but by page five it was more like a scrapbook, filled with lists of the important people in my life (1. Mum. 2. Mike. 3. Our cat) and terrible poetry ("Mike has gone and my life is / A dark page / A black night / A bottomless sea / Of / Unequalled Misery"). As soon as I get a pen in my hand, or a computer keyboard beneath my fingers, I can't stop myself, there it is, the contents of my brain in black and white, facts and fictions, thoughts, details, imaginings, everything.

And anyway, if I'm reading this in fifty years, I'll probably have forgotten things like the name of my law firm. My memory will be going, and it'll be really irritating to find that my younger self failed to record the nitpicky details of her life. So here goes.

I work at the law firm of Schuster & Marks, in New York City, on Fifty-fifth and Fifth. Today I locked my office door just before three, leaving the printer spewing out the pages of a brief I need to proofread before tomorrow morning. I flung myself through the heated revolving doors at the front of my building and out into an arctic February afternoon. Fifteen yellow cabs tooled past, their snug passengers watching, emotionlessly, the heavy pregnant woman in a sodden camel coat dancing up and down on the sparkling cold sidewalk (I forgot the important bit, I was twenty-six weeks' enceinte on Monday, yesterday). Nothing for it, I thought helplessly, as icy water prickled at my eyelashes. I pulled up my collar, clasped my hands around my enormous belly, and ran the eleven blocks uptown to my obstetrician's office through crowds of scurrying pedestrians, their faces stretched taut against the freezing wind.

Dr. Weinberg's office is as elegant as a Chelsea art gallery. Abstract lithographs in hushed silver frames decorate the waiting room. The receptionist peers out from behind a tall, slender glass vase stocked with impossible-looking South American orchids, pearly white with a faint pink flush and deep, jaundiced yellow throats. The doctor herself is an inordinately well-preserved fifty-something with high cheekbones, a narrow, burgundy mouth, and hair that seems to have suffered a serious shock mid-fluff.

After a few preliminary questions she set about prodding my stomach, pushing hard under my ribs and diaphragm. She produced a coiled fabric tape measure and measured from my pubes to just above my navel. Then she slid across the floor on her wheelie stool, leafed through the pages of a large pink file, and finally looked at me over the rim of her rectangular steel spectacles. "You're measuring small," she said.

Huh? I thought; I'm **enormous**. Children point at me in the streets. Workmen—oh-so-kindly—tell me the way to the hospital. I wear trousers with huge nylon gusset panels in the front and extra folds of elastic hidden in the waistband, and by the evening I still feel like I'm strapped into an instrument of torture.

Small? I said to her. **Small?** In relation to **what**?

She explained that the top of my uterus wasn't where it should be—i.e., halfway to my chin—and sent me for an immediate ultrasound. I called Tom (my husband, in case I develop really galloping Alzheimer's in the future) in a panic from the waiting area, but before he could leave his meeting at the Federal Courthouse I found myself in a darkened sonography room three doors down from Dr. Weinberg's office. A heavyset, expressionless woman with short graying ash-blond hair, a white coat, and loose beige trousers glanced up at me as I entered. She looked as if she'd spent most of her life underground. Her pale round face gleamed oddly in the gray-white light of a computer monitor.

"Onto the table, please," the woman said, nodding curtly at the examining couch beside her. She turned away and busied herself finding and inserting a disc into the computer, which whirred and clicked respectfully. I heaved myself up and exposed my white whale belly, feeling suddenly vulnerable, longing desperately for a bit of reassuring girly chatter ("Nothing to worry about, I'm sure, I see this all the time, it's no big deal"). No such luck. The technician squirted half a tube of thick blue sickly warm gel onto my stomach, then picked up a hard, pestle-shaped probe, without saying a word.

After forty minutes of staring at a flickering black-and-white image she told me tersely that my "fluid level" was low.

"What does that mean?" I asked the whites of her eyes.

The woman shrugged as she flicked off the monitor and ejected the disc. "Your amniotic fluid is low," she said, not entirely helpfully. "Weinberg will discuss it with you, okay?"

I wasn't sure if it was "okay" or not, but I was clearly being dismissed; the woman obviously had no intention of explaining things further and disappeared off into the corridor. The oversize door banged shut behind her. Left alone in the darkness, I wiped the slithery blue goo off my stomach with a large wad of scratchy paper from a dispenser above the couch, then pulled up my synthetic maternity trousers. "Low fluid" didn't actually sound too bad, I thought as I swung my legs carefully off the hard blue examining couch; it wasn't as if there was anything wrong with the **baby**. I'd seen him on the ultrasound screen, tiny limbs striking out, the sole of a foot flat for a second against the probe, five white toes in one perfect arc. He looked healthy to me. I returned to the doctor feeling optimistic.

Usually Dr. Weinberg looks up at me with a vague, only half-interested expression, the sort that medics always seem to wear when greeting their basically healthy patients. But this time I noticed an alertness about her, a sharpness in her face, her eyes, as if she was seeing me properly for the first time. And perhaps I was looking at her properly for the first time myself. There was a pause, and then she cleared her throat.

It was beginning to dawn on me that things weren't good.

Cherise just called me, she said, her voice deliberate and even. The baby needs amniotic fluid to develop properly, and you don't have enough of it. Either your fluid level has to rise, or we'll be delivering him fourteen weeks early.

Tom knocked at the door just in time to administer a brown paper bag. When I stopped hyperventilating, he asked the obvious question. This stuff, this amniotic stuff—**how** do we make more of it?

Bed rest, was the answer. Strict bed rest, for the duration of the pregnancy. You can lie on the sofa or in your bed, but I don't want you walking, or lifting, or even moving more than you need. One shower a day, you can sit up for dinner, come to see me, and that's it.

"The good news is, the baby seems fine so far," Dr. Weinberg said reassuringly, a flush of sympathy suddenly softening her face. "It's not all bad news, **mein bubeleh**," she added (the cover lifted, and for a second I saw the ghost of her real personality, a person at a dinner party, a mother, a sister, a daughter). "Cherise found no signs of a genetic deformity, and the baby's kidneys look healthy, so I think it's just your placenta that isn't working right. Lie on your left side to help the blood flow to the umbilical cord, and hopefully the situation will improve enough to allow him to develop quite normally. **Hopefully,**" she repeated, with meaningful emphasis. "There are no guarantees here. But you can make a big difference by obeying my directions to the letter. I don't want to run across you in the spring sale at Bloomingdale's, **versteh**?" She shooed us out with kindness. ("Come now children, chins up, you'll get through this, yes? Yes!")

As we crawled along Third Avenue in a cab toward our apartment on East Eighty-second Street, flakes of snow began whirling in the currents of air beneath the orange streetlamps like schools of tiny fish in an amber sea. Through misted icy windows I watched people rushing along the slippery sidewalks, some protecting their heads with briefcases, others holding up sodden copies of the **New York Times** with purple fingers. I tried to lean on my left side in the hard backseat, and looked over at my husband. Tom was punching messages frantically into his Black-Berry, his shoulders hunched beneath his navy wool overcoat, his spotty tie askew. He kept pushing his fingers distressfully through his curly black hair, his lips moving rapidly but silently as he typed. Feeling my eyes on him, he looked up, and he must have seen the expression on my face because he reached for my left hand and squeezed it hard. "Sorry, honey, I've got to send off these messages, I was in the middle of something when you called. Hey, hey," he added, softly, drawing me toward his shoulder, "don't look like that, don't cry! You'll be fine, the baby'll be fine, everything's going to work out, I'm sure of it." I buried my head in the dark, comforting place beneath his chin and inhaled his sweet warm smell. He held me close, whispering reassurance into my hair (**"we'll get through this, I promise..."**).

Back in our apartment, I curled up on my left side on the yellow Liberty print sofa in our sitting room. Tom emerged from our bedroom after a few moments with a blue-and-gray wool blanket, which he spread carefully over me, tucking it tightly under my toes and around my belly. Then he went into the kitchen, filled a large jug with water and ice cubes, and placed it on the teak table next to the sofa.

He stooped down to kiss me, lightly, on the forehead. "Nothing to worry about, I'm sure of it," he said once again, his voice steady as he settled himself in the leather armchair facing me. But as he turned away from my side I saw—I may be mistaken, but I **think** I saw—that his eyes were filling with tears.

2

It's now been seven hours since we left the doctor's office. We've called everyone we can think of—my mother and sisters in England, Tom's parents in Baltimore, his brother and sister-in-law in Sacramento, and an assortment of friends. I prefer to tell the story myself; as long as I'm the one describing it, I can sort of pretend to myself that I'm making it up, exaggerating for the sake of the attention. I can still be the person I thought I was twelve hours ago, a woman who had checked off at least some of the important boxes on the Modern Woman's List of Things to Do Before Hitting Thirty, that mental list all late-twenty-somethings carry around with them.

Get good job ✓
Marry handsome man with good job ✓
Have healthy bank balance ✓
Get pregnant ✓

(There are other boxes, of course, boxes I haven't managed to check or that I've had to uncheck since becoming pregnant. "Have sex three times a week," for instance. And "Be ten pounds underweight." Both of those projects are on hold for now.)

Tom's father, Peter, is a surgeon, and he sounded quite calm about the amniotic fluid thing, which made us feel slightly better until Tom pointed out that he's the kind of man who can make a **Seinfeld** joke while holding a dripping human heart in his hands. Nothing seems to rattle him, which is what you want in your surgeon but not necessarily in your father. Tom admits he spent a fair portion of his adolescence trying to get a reaction from Peter through a succession of X-treme sports—paragliding, off-piste skiing, whitewater kayaking. But none of these elicited much more than a delicately raised eyebrow, and he was on the verge of turning to more illegal means of grabbing his father's attention when a university professor suggested that he try his hand at a moot court competition. Finally he found something he enjoyed more than needling

Peter, and now he's ostensibly past his daddy hang-up, although I don't think he's as indifferent to his father's opinion as he'd like. After he told Peter about my pregnancy problem, Tom shifted the conversation delicately to the subject of "My Many and Varied Successes at Work." He's going up for partner soon at his law firm, one of the biggest in the city, and from the way he described it you'd think he was a shoo-in. This isn't **completely** true. He's got an excellent chance, I'm sure of it, but only a tiny percentage of associates make the final cut.

Then he spoke to his mother, a brief conversation conducted in the staccato tones of two people who lack the affection for each other that rounds and softens the voice. She's a thin, uptight Boston Brahmin who's never quite forgiven Tom for not being a girl through whom she could relive her years as a willowy debutante. "I was **sure** he was going to be a girl," I once heard her say to a friend over a cup of Lapsang souchong. "He was lying sideways in the womb, after all," she added, casting him a reproachful look. She's received the news of Tom's various academic and legal successes over the years with the half-glazed look of one who'd rather be attending to her tea roses.

At the moment Tom is dashing about in our tiny kitchen. He's hurling slices of ham into some hacked-up pieces of cranberry-walnut bread while yelling into the speakerphone, trying to rearrange a work trip while periodically rushing over to kiss me apologetically and hiss contritely in my ear—"have to explain things to these guys, Q, so sorry, but your dinner's almost ready…"

(I've been "Q" to everyone, friends and family, for as long as I can remember. Someone at school noticed that the character "Q" in the Bond movies is really called Major Boothroyd; my last name is Boothroyd, my first name is Quinn, **et voilà tout**. I rather like it. I may be a boringly respectable married lawyer but I sound like the sort of popstrel who drives a pearly SUV with bulletproof windows and champagne-soaked seats.)

I called my office as soon as we got back from the doctor's, and after some initial bewilderment ("amni-**what**?") and a few very long pauses, Fay—one of Schuster's partners—agreed to divide my cases among the other senior associates. From now on I'm relieved of all duties, doctor's orders ("I don't want any teleconferencing from home, you hear me? Cut all ties to the office. Stress can divert blood away from the baby").

Three months away from the office is not, let's face it, a disaster. Life as a New York lawyer is certainly better paid than life as a London lawyer, but I can't say the job is everything I dreamed it would be when I upped and left England four years ago. The work is just as mind-numbing, and the hours are considerably longer. Tom and I pass each other in the bathroom at 6 A.M. most days and meet up occasionally on Sunday evenings for a picnic in Central Park. How we conceived a child is a mystery neither of us can solve—or could solve, if we ever found the time to talk about it. I sort of remember a passionate fumble after a black-tie affair to welcome the summer associates at his firm. We flirted outrageously through the main course, groped each other drunkenly under the table during dessert, fell into a taxi cab at two, and I think we made love on the kitchen table when we got home, although I can't be sure. But I like to think that's when we conceived our baby, rather than during one of our more conscientious couplings, the sort that occur simply because both of us happen to be home before eleven.

So at least the next three months will give me the chance to get to know Tom properly again; we love each other, but I've been conscious of something happening between us these last few months, a new space opening up, like the dark water between a boat and its mooring. It's nothing serious, of course, not a real separation; I'm not talking affairs, threats of divorce, that sort of thing. Certainly not. In fact, on our occasional days together the gap closes completely, vanishing over brunch in the West Village and a leisurely wander through Washington Square, where we first met four years ago. Then a week later I'm suddenly conscious of it again. I catch one of us in an ungenerous moment—a scratchy comment, a self-righteous criticism, a thoughtless act, the kind of thing we'd never have done, or said, or even thought when we first got together.

Partly it's the long hours at work, partly it's the pregnancy. For a man, the nine months of pregnancy pass pretty much like any other nine months of an adult's life; Tom can refer to "when the baby arrives" as if it's not already here in the room with us, aiming lusty kicks into the depths of my stomach. **My** life changed completely within a week of discovering that I was pregnant. One day I was staring delightedly at the second line on a small gray plastic pen, the next I was depositing my dinner into the toilet and discovering that the stairs between the two floors of my office had unaccountably turned into K2.

Bed rest should give us an opportunity to close the gap permanently before the baby comes. Maybe (who knows!) we'll even get round to fucking for a change. I've hardly been at my sexiest these last few months; I've been crawling into bed too exhausted to brush my teeth, much less perform my **Glamour**-reader-sex-kitten routine. Lying on my side for the next fourteen weeks will at least let me catch up on some sleep—although, thinking about it, I'm not sure it's the ideal kick start for a lagging sex life. **Hi honey, I've spent the last thousand hours staring at daytime TV, d'you wanna get it on?** And are we even **allowed** to have sex while I'm on bed rest? Dr. Weinberg didn't say anything about it, but surely it diverts blood away from the uterus—or is it diverted **to** the uterus? Must remember to look up that one on the Web tomorrow.

There are other things I need to research online, this whole condition for starters. I'd barely heard of amniotic fluid until today. And prematurity, better look up that one as well, I completely passed over the section on "The Premature Child" in **Yes! You're Having a Baby.** Fourteen weeks early sounds like one of those tiny creatures you see on the March of Dimes ads, little alien beings with translucent skin and fingers the size of pine needles. I can hardly bear to think of it. I think I'll try Googling "26 weeks' gestation"—

Lots of hits for "26 weeks." Prematurebabies. com informs me that babies born at this developmental stage are at risk for some pretty nasty conditions. But here's the good news. By thirty weeks, their chances of survival are close to 90 percent and the risk of a serious illness drops dramatically. So I **have** to do everything I can to make more of this fluid stuff, I have to keep him safe inside me for at least four more weeks. That's just four weeks of lying on my left side 24/7. Really, when you think about it, that doesn't sound so bad. Does it?

3

Wednesday 11:05 A.M.

This is the first morning of my first full day on bed rest. I think I'm doing great. My sister Jeanie said last night on the telephone that I'd be bored into depression within twenty-four hours, but Jeanie is the kind of person who can't occupy herself for a nanosecond. When we were kids she was always trailing after me and Alison, trying to persuade us to play with her and screaming the house down when we wouldn't. I'm the oldest of the three of us, and I've always been the best at keeping myself entertained.

So far this morning I have:

- Checked my Yahoo e-mail. Twice. Okay, a few more times than that.
- Read the **New York Times, including** the business section.
- Checked the updated **Times** on the Web.
- Paid the bills. Even the scarily huge ones.

(High on the Modern Woman's List of Things to Do Before Hitting Thirty is "Stop hiding credit card bills furtively in back issues of **Cosmopolitan**" and "Read more than just the Metro section of the **Times**." I don't think I can honestly check those boxes just yet, but I'm eyeing them with a new feeling of optimism.)

And I haven't switched on the TV once! Alison claimed I'd be addicted to **Days of Our Lives** before the end of the week, but so far I've found plenty to do without resorting to soaps and chat shows. Although I might watch **Ricki Lake** this afternoon at five. Today's topic is almost relevant to me—it's about getting pregnant, anyway.

Tom hurled himself out the door at 7 A.M., then rushed back in at 7:05 in a panic, threw a piece of cheese in between two slices of bread and left it on the table beside the sofa ("I'm sorry, honey, I forgot, shit, I'm SO late—"). This, apparently, is my lunch. I'm tempted to order something for delivery, but then I'll have to get up to answer the door—

3:20 P.M.

The lunch problem was solved by Brianna, this crazy paralegal from work. We started working together on a case about a month ago. We aren't particularly close, but she came steaming uptown during her lunch hour with, would you believe, spicy pepperoni pizza and a lightly tossed garden salad in tow. I've decided I'll have to answer the door to visitors—I'll go mad if I don't—but once I'd let Brianna in I lay virtuously on the sofa wolfing down pizza while she sat on the red Persian kilim that runs the width of our sitting room and told me about her tangled love life and the painful plight of the paralegal (eight months ago she quit the Manhattan U.S. attorney's office for Schuster, where she gets better pay but worse treatment).

I've had five calls from the office since Brianna left, all work related. Nothing I can't handle. Fortunately I'd already started putting together notes on all my files in preparation for maternity leave. My work in-box is bound to be brimming by now, but I've decided to ignore it—once they realize I'm not checking they'll have to leave me alone. The office already seems strangely distant, another world, another life.

One hour and forty minutes to **Ricki**. What shall I do now?

3:50 P.M.

At least the sitting room window faces my sofa. I can watch the sky and see the weather, that most English of pleasures. If I crane really hard I can glimpse people walking along the sidewalks at the intersection of Eighty-second and Second. And I can also see the inhabitants of the small 1940s apartment building opposite, the two uppermost floors anyway.

The window I'm staring out of is rectangular and very large (the real estate agent who showed us around called it a "stunning focal point," which translated means the room itself is just a plain oblong box). There's a wooden radiator bench underneath it that's just about wide enough to sit on. We've propped a few chenille cushions on top, and it's a great place to settle with a book (well, it would be, if we ever had the time). Around the window we've hung heavy red curtains that graze the wooden floors from a long iron pole. A few weeks after we moved in, on a rare day off from work, I unearthed a cranberry glass vase to match in an antiques shop around the corner. It lives on the Danish teak table beside the sofa, and when the light shines through, an intense red stain appears on the wood behind it, like a spilled glass of pinot noir. A distressed brown leather armchair stands in the right-hand corner of the room, at an angle, facing me. Along the yellow-painted wall on the left there are two bookcases. The one nearest the window, filled with a jumble of undergraduate textbooks and embossed John Grisham paperbacks, mostly from airport book-shops, belongs to Tom. Mine, which stands closer to the sofa, contains a chronological collection of poetry books, essays, and novels from Austen to Atwood. It's also decorated with a few family photographs in wooden frames and some English sea-smoothed glass.

The room is small (this is Manhattan after all), but it's bright and cozy. The radiator is going full blast; I can see ripples of heat in the air above the bench. I don't think I've spent more than ten hours total in my sitting room since the day we moved in. But it's become my world for the rest of my pregnancy.

The building opposite will be gone later in the year; apparently, it's going to be knocked down and replaced with something bigger and more modern. I heard somewhere—from two people talking in the elevator, or was it by the mailboxes—that it has terrible mold. From what I can see (and if I strain I can see right into the rooms), most of the residents are elderly, many of them even octogenarians; I've been observing them trotting slowly backward and forward, passing from room to room, for much of the last hour. They seem to be living in a different time zone from the rest of us, every movement measured, every step careful. I watched as an elderly gentleman in the corner apartment tried to replace a lightbulb. It took him about five minutes to get up his little stepladder. When he reached the top it shook wildly, he dropped the bulb, and then he had to start all over again. It was quite entertaining. The lady in the apartment next to him is just watching TV in the semidarkness.

6:02 P.M.

Shit—I missed the end of **Ricki** (got to love Ricki) because Alison decided to call in the middle, so now I'll never know if Erik or Vinnie fathered Tay-sha's baby. Officially Alison phoned to see how I was doing. Unofficially she called to gloat.

"You have to promise me you'll take it easy from now on," she cooed. She was positively ooz-ing smug satisfaction. "Pregnancy is really tough on your body, Q—believe me, I know! I tried to do what you did when I was pregnant with Geof-frey, but I realized in time you've got to make con-cessions to your growing baby's needs. The hours you work, it's just ridiculous! It's one thing for Tom to stay up 'til all hours, but it isn't reason-able for a woman in your condition. I think this was a wake-up call for you, Q, I really do."

Then I had to listen for twenty minutes while Alison drivelled on about how you have to pay at-tention to your body's signals, how the pregnant woman's body is a delicate blooming flower, and how she and my mother were saying **only last week** that I'd come to grief unless I cut back my hours. She says she lay awake last night worrying about me and the baby. I think she hasn't had this much fun in ages.

Alison's had this "thing" about me for years, this second sibling thing. When we were children she had to do whatever I did, only better. She pretty much kept up until we got to university, but then she finally realized there were things she could do that I couldn't—acting, being cool, dat-ing luscious men with handles to their name—

and she became a lot happier. And a lot more impossible.

I remember the sick, miserable expression on her face the day I got my GCSE results at sixteen—all As. She worked like an absolute demon the next year to prepare for her own exams; in fact, she gave herself carpal tunnel syndrome and spent six months in physical therapy. And I remember the spark of hope, perhaps even of triumph, in her eyes the day I found out I failed to get the expected A in my physics A-level. The funny thing was, she was better at physics than I, but she got a B herself the next year. I don't know whether she lost her motivation, or if—and this is what Tom thinks—she couldn't actually deal with the idea of beating me. I mean, her whole life had been spent trying to one-up me, then the opportunity presented itself, and she bottled out.

Anyway, like me she got into Oxford at the last minute, like me she read PPE—politics, philosophy, economics—but unlike me she checked out in her second year and took the starring role in **Guess Who's Coming to Dinner** instead. She took to wearing black jeans, black turtlenecks, and secondhand suede jackets from Camden Market. She dyed her hair blond and scrunched it up into these devastating little glossy rolls, secured at the nape of her neck with a lacquered chopstick. And she dated a long line of devilishly handsome actors (who also wore black jeans and black turtlenecks, and who affected just-rolled-out-of-bed hairdos). She became a social "hit" in a way I never was. I spent my years at university trailing solo up and down the Woodstock Road with half-a-hundred-weight of books under my arm, while she acted nightly to great acclaim, grades dropping through the floor, but she didn't give a damn. We'd meet for sandwich lunches in the Covered Market, and she'd show up with a packet of Camels lodged in her hipster pockets (this was before she decided her body was a blooming flower, you understand) and inform me I had no idea how to **live**. I don't mind admitting, I almost lost my head—I was so used to trying to stay one step ahead of her that I didn't know what to do with myself when she opted out of the system and settled for a Third class degree. I tried attending a few of her parties—usually held in dark smoky basements among piles of half-painted scenery—but if there's one thing guaranteed to humiliate, it's being the egghead older sibling of a talented nubile sexpot. I decided to leave her to it and went back to my books.

While I was doing my law conversion course in London, she got together with Greg and had yet another change of heart. Acting was all very well, she told me, but it's a draining profession, hardly consistent with serious relationships. She'd met Greg while rehearsing **Caligula**; he was one of the tousled actors with a suspiciously implausible cockney accent. Sure enough, it turned out the closest he'd ever got to the East End was Liverpool Street Station, en route to the family stately home in North Norfolk. The Honorable Gregory Farquhar had no intention of spending his life with a bunch of poverty-stricken actors, and as soon as he graduated (barely) from Oxford, he hotfooted it to the city, where he now earns pots of money working for one of daddy's chums. Greg, let's face it, was something of a catch, and Alison knew it. They were married at twenty-two (wedding covered briefly in the pages of **Hello!**), and Alison quit acting to work on her sculpture. Translation: Alison became a baby machine. She's produced two so far, and she's itching to get started on number three.

So yes, she does have more experience in the baby-making department than I do, and she'll never let me forget it. Ever since Geoffrey's appearance three years ago, she's been extolling the joys of motherhood (the last time she came out to see me she saw my Pills on the bedside table and shook her head so dolefully that you'd have thought they were class-A drugs). "Motherhood is such a bond between women, Q," she told me with that dreadful yogic light in her eye. (She wears Gaultier these days and has a three-quarters-of-a-million-pound pad in Pimlico, and her very own spiritual counselor to help her find enlightenment in the midst of it all.) "It would be so wonderful to be able to share my experiences of maternity with you! And I do want our children to be in the same age-range, I want them to view each other as close friends, not just relatives—don't you, Q?" Truth is, Geoffrey and Serena are the kind of children I hope my kids run screaming from. Greg likes to see his son and heir in sailor suits, and Serena spends most days in a pink tutu telling anyone who'll listen that she wants to be a "pwincess" when she grows up. I really hope we have a kick-ass daughter at some point who'll take Serena behind a bush, and—

Well anyway, the idea of Alison's doing "what I did" when she was pregnant with Geoffrey is laughable; since she's been married to Greg she's barely done a serious day's work. She has her very own studio (bought by hubbie, of course), and from what I can tell, she wanders in three days a week for a few hours and comes out with a pot with no bottom, or something equally ridiculous. She gets to think she's a serious artiste because Greg's cousin is an art dealer, who knows a guy, who knows another guy, who owns some art space in south London, so every three years or so I get a chic little white card inviting me to an exhibition of Alison Farquhar's work, puffed up by some obsequious chump from the **Evening Standard** (also a friend of hubbie's, no doubt). But of course I can't say any of this when Alison blathers on about understanding the pressures of work, can I—!

4

Thursday 10:30 A.M.

Rereading yesterday's diary entry, it strikes me I am not (as the therapist I briefly visited last year might remark) altogether "resolved" about Alison. I must think more about this. "Be effortlessly superior to younger sisters" is an important item on the Modern Woman's List of Things to Do Before Hitting Thirty.

I was still fairly wound up when Tom got home at ten, not to mention consumed with the pregnant woman's desperate, slavering need for **food**. He'd been "on the verge" of leaving the office since six, and by the time he actually appeared I was seething with hunger, anger, and frustration. Five minutes after he walked through the door I was throwing the sofa cushions, screaming and crying because he hadn't picked up takeout on the way home and now I was going to have to wait **another half hour** before my supper arrived.

In the midst of all the yelling and throwing and general carrying-on I caught sight of the expression on Tom's face. Thirty-six hours ago he had a moderately normal woman for a wife—true, she has an accent that makes half of New York swoon and the other half think of Cruella De Vil, not to mention a belly that (as I might have mentioned) causes dogs to back away in fright. But apart from that, she was pretty normal. Now, in the space of a day, she's turned into a whirling dervishing Tasmanian devil. My husband pulled at his curly black hair in a rather desperate way as he watched his caged wife froth and fume.

I stopped crying when he suddenly sank to his knees by the sofa and muttered something about "conserving fluid." Almost in spite of myself, I reached out for the nape of his neck and pushed my hand through his fine dark hair. Then, after a bit more hiccupping and moaning (just to get my point across), I picked up the phone book from the bottom shelf of the side table, chucked it in his direction, and told him to find me some food, and fast. After all, it **was** ten o'clock.

Now it's Bed Rest Day Two, and Tom and I have instituted some changes to our routine:

- He'll come home within half an hour of when he says he's coming home so I'm not stuck in a twilight limbo.
- I'll order the food in the evening for him to pick up from a restaurant of my choice.
- He will make/buy me a sandwich I actually want to eat for lunch and leave it in a cooler by the sofa, and he'll also leave a bowl of fruit and some nuts for snacking. (I was

tempted to add, and a packet of chocolate chip cookies, but I'll be rolling to the hospital in fourteen weeks if I'm not careful.)
- He will try to understand what it's like to be stuck at home all day, and I'll try to remember that he's worried, too (blah blah blah).
- I Will Not Let Alison Get to Me.

This all seems pretty reasonable. My mozzarella and artichoke pesto sandwich is on the side table—well, what's left of it, I ate half of it at eight-thirty this morning—and I've already decided on the menu for this evening. This city is bristling with fabulous restaurants, and I have three months to work my way through them. Armed with my trusty Zagat and a few back issues of the **New York Times** food section I'll have the next dozen-or-so suppers mapped out in no time.

4 P.M.

Brianna has been here again, which was a good thing, because the mozzarella sandwich was finished by eleven. I was starting to freak, actually, about how I was going to make two kiwi fruit and a packet of dry roasted peanuts last for nine hours. Then Bri shows up with four slices of thin-crust pizza from La Margherita round the corner. After I'd consumed three of them she took the hint and rustled up a ham and cheese omelette in the kitchen. **And** she brought me some chocolate chip cookies, for which I thanked her abjectly. I ate one immediately, and I'm saving the other to eat while watching Ricki this afternoon.

In return for her generosity I had to listen to yet more tedious details about her love life. As my mother would say, she's not a high-wattage bulb. She's been having an affair with a married man for the last year or so and seems bamboozled by lines like "I have to stay for the sake of the children" and "I'd marry you tomorrow, but my wife's on antidepressants." I thought they stopped making women like that in the 1950s.

If you ask me she's the kind of girl men have affairs with but never marry. She's got fabulous cleavage and long slender legs, and she's pretty enough; she has long straight dark hair and a smattering of unexpected freckles across her nose. Her mother is from an old Italian family that apparently once owned several snug villas and a fair-size olive grove in the hills above Florence, then lost it all in the years after the Second World War. Her father's family were impoverished Irish immigrants who made good as shipbuilders on their arrival in the New World. But despite (or perhaps because of) the lineage she has a sort of simple feyness, an innocent "come-take-advantage-of-me" air that I can imagine some men find irresistible. When I suggested that married people have a nasty habit of staying married her dark eyes widened ever so slightly. "He wants to leave his wife," she assured me, earnestly. "He just has to find the right time, you know?" She swooshed her curtain of hair over her shoulder with a delicate flick of the wrist.

After Bri left, I began surfing the Web for information on my condition—it has a nice long name, oligohydramnios—and I've ordered subscriptions to various magazines, a mix of the worthy (**The Economist, Time**) and the not-so-worthy (**Vogue, Harper's, Glamour**, and, on a whim, something called **Working Mother**. After clicking the subscribe button I had a panic about whether I was ever going to be a working mother, but then I have to live positively.)

6:15 P.M.

Why do people disturb me halfway through **Ricki? Just** as I'm settling down to enjoy "I Was a 'Ho But Now I'm a Hottie" the phone rings or the doorbell goes, and that's the end of that.

Today it was Fay from work. She's brusque and short, with glossy cropped brown hair, friendly enough, but always deathly preoccupied by work. Frankly, I was amazed to see her here. I think Brianna must have said something, because she showed up with a bag of cookies—not, I'm afraid to say, a bag of chocolate chip cookies, but a bag of raisin oatmeal cookies. I do not like raisin oatmeal cookies. What I particularly hate about raisin oatmeal cookies is that they look like chocolate chip cookies from a distance. I get my hopes up. And then they are dashed.

So I was grumpy as soon as she arrived, and I got a whole lot grumpier when she off-loaded some dreadfully earnest hardcover book on me. "I've been meaning to read this fucking thing for ages," she said brightly, "but I never get the god-damn time. So now **you** have the time, you can read it for me and tell me all about it. **Hahaha-haha!**"

Not funny. Not funny at all. I have plenty of earnest books on my own bookshelf. What makes her think I want to read her earnest book for her? I have nowhere to go, nothing else to do, and the woman wants to turn my life into a living hell?

I didn't say this, of course. I said, how lovely, I'll be really interested to read about one woman's solo trek through the Andes in the face of a diagnosis of terminal cancer. Oh, and she has a prosthetic limb as well. Marvelous. Can't wait to get started.

After that, Fay talked work for about an hour—she doesn't have anything else to talk about be-cause, as far as I can tell, she doesn't **do** anything else. She broke up with her long-term girlfriend two years ago and says she hasn't dated since. She's already been made a partner, but she's at the office even longer hours than I am. She's gone back there now and probably won't leave 'til after midnight. What a horrible, lonely, miserable life.

5

Friday Noon

Day three of bed rest. I woke up this morning and thought, This may go on for another ninety days. And I burst into tears.

But I pulled myself together by the time Tom left for work, to his evident relief ("I can't go to the office and leave you like this!"), and I've just spent a vigorous hour plucking my eyebrows into submission. I have also:

- waxed my belly (the hairs have taken to growing thick and dark on my navel, and if I'm going to be inspected every five minutes for the next thirteen and a half weeks I might as well be looking my best);
- taken a nap (woke up to find I'd drooled all over our red chenille throw cushion—why do pregnant women drool so much? Is it so they'll be better prepared for their babies' slobber?);

- watched an old lady in the opposite building clean her floors (all the ones I could see, anyway);
- cracked and called my mother.

The last, I'll admit, was a mistake. It's one thing to call my mother to impart information (Alison's flight's arriving at 7:10, I'm sending you an article from **The New Yorker,** I have low amniotic fluid and our baby may be delivered prematurely). It's another thing entirely to call for comfort or support.

So the conversation went something like this:

ME: Hi, Mum, how're you doing? I'm going a little crazy here, stuck on my left side day after day! Thought I'd call for some cheering up.

HER: Well, I don't want to say it's your own fault…. Have you tried ylang-ylang?

ME: My own fault? How is this my fault?

HER: I don't want to say this wouldn't have happened if you lived in England…

ME: What do you mean? How has this got anything to do with where I live? This has nothing to do with where I live!

HER: I said I **didn't** want to tell you it had something to do with moving to America—

ME: You think this is all about my hours, don't you? Here we go **again**! You think I'd be working less hard in London, and that all my problems are caused by the crazy American work ethic. You don't actually know anything about lawyers' hours in London, or about the American work ethic, but you still think you—

HER: Actually I **do** know something about this, madam! Jane Cooper's daughter works five days a week and is home in time to pick up her kids from school....

ME: Jane Cooper's daughter is a bloody paralegal in Saffron Walden, the two are hardly comparable—

HER: There's no need to swear, dear; you called **me,** remember, and I don't have to listen to your rudeness....

The conversation ended some forty minutes later, after I had (a) conceded that I was probably working too hard and (b) agreed to try ylang-ylang on my pillow at night. This inspired a half-hour meltdown on my part after I put down the phone; why do I, a moderately successful, fairly self-confident lawyer, routinely lose these kinds of battles with my mother? Why do I find myself red-faced and tearful when she tells me I've done something wrong? Why does it **matter** to me that she thinks

I've done something wrong? I long to be the kind of person who can laugh lightly, with an air of indulgence, at her mother's foibles. I long to be the kind of person who can check the box that says "have superbly adult relationship with mother" on the Modern Woman's List of Things to Do Before Hitting Thirty. But I am not this person.

Anyway, the various hair-pulling activities gave me a constructive outlet for my venom, and it's about time for Brianna to show up with some lunchtime bit of deliciousness.

2 P.M.

No Brianna. But that's okay, Tom left a mound of sandwiches made with outrageously expensive cheese from Zabar's (he made a guilt-inspired shopping dash on his way home from work yesterday afternoon to buy me my favorite English cheese, crumbly white Cheshire—"Here you are, Q, don't say I never get you anything good, by the way I might have to work late tomorrow..."). And I still have those damn raisin oatmeal cookies that Fay brought. If I pick out all the raisins (nasty wrinkly things) they'll do as my treat for this afternoon.

6

Monday 10 A.M.

Why is no one coming to see me? I've had at least
a dozen phone calls from people at the office either explaining why they **can't** come, or offering
vague promises of visits in the future (when the
kids have gotten over their colds, when the trial
finishes, when they get back from the Maldives).
You'd think I lived in upstate New York, not in
the middle of the city. How hard is it to hop on
the subway? True, Lara and Mark dropped in for
lunch on Sunday, but that's a delight I'd be happy
to pass up. I'm not a fan of either of them: Mark
was in law school with Tom, but he's become absolutely terrifying since he became an assistant U.S.
attorney and started pursuing lowly ganja deal-
ers; Lara is an insanely toned gym instructor who
seems to have given birth to their two children
through her nose for all the effect it's had on her
figure. She looks at my flabby floppy belly with
barely disguised distaste. They're also the worst
guests in the hemisphere. Okay, so they brought
takeout, but would it have hurt them to help Tom
tidy up a bit afterward? This place is a sty! And
they didn't bring me any treats, just a damn bottle
of chardonnay, which I can't drink, for obvious
reasons. Not a slice of cake or cookie in sight.

Weirdly enough, the nicest visit I had was from this funny little Greek lady who lives in one of the apartments downstairs. She knocked on the door Saturday afternoon and asked if she could take a look at our apartment; she's involved in some kind of fight with our landlord about the services he provides, and she wanted to compare our apartment with hers. Anyway, half an hour after she'd examined the kitchen appliances and the state of the air-conditioning units she showed up again with a dish of homemade moussaka and a paper plate of sweetmeats made from semolina. Her English is far from perfect (her accent is heavy and thick as honey), but she was incredibly kind. She said she'd come again soon with homemade baklava, which is **almost** as good as a chocolate chip cookie.

So here I am again, beginning of a new week, the end of my first on bed rest. I'm twenty-seven weeks' pregnant. If the baby was born today he'd be thirteen weeks' premature. I just Googled "twenty-seven weeks gestation survival" and found a Web site that claims his chances are already around 85 percent! Feel hugely cheered.

11 A.M.

I just Googled "oligohydramnios survival" and "low amniotic fluid prognosis." Big mistake, Q. Big, gynormous mistake.

I've been sucking at a paper bag for the last twenty minutes, but I still can't stop crying. An average twenty-seven week baby may have an 85 percent chance of making it, but babies in low fluid may do a great deal worse. Second trimester oligohydramnios has "a poor prognosis," apparently; lung development "may be fatally retarded." Children who seem healthy in their mother's wombs may die on delivery because of something called **pulmonary hypoplasia**.

Once I discovered this, I felt compelled to find out more. And soon I found myself reading chat room posts from women across the country who were advised to terminate their pregnancies when oligohydramnios was diagnosed. Whose babies suffocated at birth because their lungs couldn't function. Whose children were born with an appalling mix of physical and mental deformities.

I threw up in the bathroom a few minutes ago; since then I've been shaking on the sofa. I'm trying to get control of myself by writing this. Why didn't my doctor tell me about pulmonary hypoplasia? Did she think I wouldn't be able to cope? Actually, I don't know if I **can** cope. How am I going to get through the next five, ten weeks not knowing if this baby is going to live?

12 P.M.

In desperation, I called Dr. Weinberg's office. The kindly receptionist brought my appointment forward from tomorrow afternoon to today, at four. I've told Tom he has to leave work to take me. He wasn't pleased ("Christ, Q, I'm up to my eyeballs, hell I'm over them"), but then I started crying hysterically, telling him everything I'd just read, and he went very quiet. That made me even more terrified—I wanted him to tell me that I was being stupid, that you can't believe everything you read on the Web. But he didn't. He was just very, very quiet, and I could hear him breathing slowly and hard the way he does when he's trying to stay calm. "Jesus," he said at last, half under his breath.

I can't eat, but I've been drinking water feverishly these last few hours ("Keep hydrated," Dr. Weinberg told me last week. Does that mean the water I drink will get to the baby somehow? How can that be? How does it get from my stomach to my womb?)

3:30 P.M.

Tom will be here any minute. But I'm calmer now.

The little Greek lady came by with the plate of baklava. I was weeping miserably when she pushed the doorbell, and I wasn't planning on answering it, but she must have heard me because she called urgently through the door to ask if anything was wrong. I thought about telling her to go away, and frankly I still don't quite know why I didn't. But, for whatever reason, I got up and opened the door. She took one look at me, led me back to the sofa, and told me to lie down again.

She immediately saw I hadn't eaten my lunch, so she broke off small pieces from my sandwich and fed them to me one at a time. I discovered I was extremely hungry and ate them obediently, like a small child. Afterward she gave me some of the baklava with a glass of milk. "This difficult time," she said to me, at last, very seriously, "but you try to stay peaceful. No point thinking bad thoughts, you fight them, you know? Good girl, eh? Good girl." Then, to my surprise, she dropped a maternal kiss on my cheek as she got up to leave. "See you soon, I come with more things, sweet wholesome things, you eat yourself to good health, yes?" She gurgled with sudden, irrepressible laughter. "I come back see you soon, I promise."

She mentioned in passing today that she doesn't have kids; I wonder why not. She would have made a great mother.

7 P.M.

I'm back home after the appointment, ensconced on the yellow print sofa once more. Tom has had to go back to the office.

I wish I felt completely better, I wish I felt 100 percent comforted after our meeting with Dr. Weinberg. I want to feel the way I did a week or two ago, like a simple healthy animal, a cow perhaps, giving birth without giving the matter a thought. Now everything seems so complicated, a matter of tests and diagnoses, of readings in centimeters (or is it millimeters?), of charts, diagrams, statistics.

To be fair, things could've been worse.

We got to Dr. Weinberg's consulting rooms a few minutes early. The waiting room was filled with pregnant women, their hands resting lightly on their rounded bellies. Last week, I was one of the women with a beatific Madonna smile. This week, I slunk into the corner and hid my "small" abdomen behind a copy of the **New York Times**. I felt so inadequate.

First I had another ultrasound. Cherise was waiting in her small shadowed room for me, probe in hand. "I remember you," she said coolly when I walked in. "I suppose we'll be seeing a lot of you from now on," she added, cracking open her tube and slithering my belly with sickly warm goo. I shivered.

And yet what a relief to see the baby once more on the screen, the four chambers of the heart clearly visible, each one tiny, distinct, perfect. And what a strange, mysterious delight to see his skeleton in motion. Delicately contoured tibia and fibula flashed left and right; the stacked column of his vertebrae undulated as he flipped up and down and around, twisting about his umbilical cord like a fairground gymnast around a rope. A face flashed into view for a second, and something about his cheeks, about the structure of bone around his eyes, reminded me of my father. How funny, I thought. All these years my dad has been dead, a part of him has been living inside of me waiting to be reborn.

Cherise seemed to be in an uncharacteristically expansive mood today, because she told me at the end of the session that my fluid level was "stable; not much change here." I still don't have enough of the stuff, apparently, but at least I haven't lost any since last week.

Then we saw the doctor, who started out by scolding me for reading Web posts on my condition. What kind of **mishegoss** is this? She waggled her finger severely. I was quite glad to be scolded, actually—it had a ring of the "don't believe everything you read" stump I wanted from Tom this morning. She then said that my oligohydramnios was not "severe," and that pulmonary hypoplasia only develops when amniotic fluid levels are lower than mine. But she doesn't rule it out entirely either. And if the baby does have it, there's nothing whatsoever we can do. There's no test they can administer to assess the baby's lung development. It's just a question of wait and see.

I was staring miserably at the linoleum floor during all of this, and Tom was gazing with unfocused eyes out of the discreetly shaded windows. Dr. Weinberg must have seen how distressed we were because she picked up the pace of the conversation and said, "Listen, your baby's anatomical growth appears to be on track, I haven't seen signs of physical damage—babies who don't have enough room often develop club feet, and that's easy to spot—so there's every reason to be optimistic. I can't pretend we might not find something on delivery, something we haven't seen on the ultrasound, but I think he's going to come out of this well. Take it a week at a time," she added, turning to look straight at me. "And cut out the Web surfing, yes? After all, who posts a story to say, I had a scare, but everything turned out okay? Remember, if you have further questions ask **me,** not freakedoutmomma@yahoo.com.

"And you," she said, turning to Tom with a shade of reproof on her angular face, "keep her calm, yes? Your job is to keep her going, keep her comfortable. Lots of foot rubs and treats, yes?" Tom gave her a brief, pained smile and muttered something about the pressures of work.

But I think he took her advice to heart because when we got home he dashed out and returned a quarter of an hour later with a huge vitamin-enriched milkshake (tons of protein, good for fetal development), a bag of chips, and a couple of DVDs. He's had to go back to the office for a meeting with a client, but at least I have something to keep me occupied. I do miss him, though. I wish he was here to watch the movies with me. I'm starting to feel terribly lonely.

7

Tuesday 10 A.M.

Tom's been at work for over three hours already, but so far I've managed to avoid surfing the Web for more scare stories about my condition. Instead I have:

• eaten three pieces of baklava.

That's about it, actually. Other than that I've stared out the window at yet another gray, cool, slushy East Coast morning and watched an elderly gentleman in the apartment complex opposite bang on his TV to try and get it to work. Then I went through my address book to see if there's anyone I'd like to talk to (there isn't) and napped for twenty minutes. It feels like six weeks since I first went on bed rest. How can it be only eight days?

10:45 A.M.

Still can't think of anything to do—except panic.
I have to turn my thoughts in a new direction. I'm
going to call my mother. This is almost certainly a
mistake. I'm going to do it anyway.

11:30 A.M.

Well, that wasn't too bad, all things considering.
She was in a good mood because the yoga studio's
profits are up this quarter.

To be fair, she has been a lot happier generally since she retired from her "proper" job as a
bank manager and opened the studio. I wasn't as
supportive as I might have been when she first
told me the plan; frankly I thought she was turning into a cliché of the single woman, complete
with floaty kaftans, incense, and a slightly wild
hairdo. Now I think she looks quite nice in the
kaftans, she reserves the incense for special occa-
sions, and crazy hairstyle notwithstanding, she's
making a good job of the business. In the space
of a few years she's turned it into a profit-making
enterprise: all credit to her, she spotted a niche in
the market—to wit, women over sixty with plenty of spare time who don't want to creak their
limbs in front of bendy twentysome-things. I've
never been to one of her classes, but Jeanie says
they're a riot—a dozen-odd blue-rinses in deck

shoes and sweatpants, giggling like mad when they can't hold "the cat." They love my mother, apparently—funny that she's so tolerant and forgiving of other people's shortcomings when mine assume the shape of heinous crimes.

I often wonder what would have happened if my father hadn't walked out when I was thirteen. Of course, she might have chucked him out herself, eventually. He was my dad, and I loved him, but he was one of the most ineffectual men to walk the face of the earth. He spent most of my childhood trying to be a songwriter—trying, and conspicuously failing. True, he played the piano beautifully, and he had a wonderful voice; I vividly recall him singing war songs ("If You Were the Only Girl in the World," "Roses in Picardy," "We'll Meet Again") to me and my sisters when we were in the bath. Not, I hasten to add, that he'd actually served in the army; he missed the Second World War by a few years, which was probably a good thing, because he couldn't fight his way out of a paper bag as my mother used to say. He spent half his life on the dole, the other half shuttling between low-level temporary jobs—gardener, substitute teacher, children's entertainer (my bendy balloon dog collection was the envy of all my friends). And then, when I was about twelve, he started this desperate, pathetic affair with the next-door neighbor, a woman who'd spent her entire life in curlers and slippers, cleaning other people's houses, but longing to be a classical guitar teacher of all things. They moved to Brighton, and I hardly saw him again. He died of a heart attack when I was in my first year at university.

I've always suspected that if he'd stayed my mother would have had less energy to devote to scolding her three daughters. We certainly became conscious of the force of her will in the years after he left. She was determined we should take after her, not him—**stability** and **security** were to be our watchwords, she told us. She wanted us all to have a good university education, preferably at Oxford (she was the first in her family to go to university, but in her day the city of aquatint was out of reach for a workingman's daughter, so she wound up at Southampton). After that she wanted to see us comfortably ensconced in one of "the professions," the taint of the yeomanry finally erased from the family. I was right on target, an A-plus daughter, until I took a job in the States—that **wasn't** part of Mummy's plan. As far as my mother is concerned, America is a country of crooks and charlatans, shady types dressed in spats and low-brimmed fedoras. I keep inviting her to visit, but she always declines; I don't think she'd know what to do if she discovered New Yorkers don't actually congregate in speakeasies and plunge their enemies into concrete vats.

And now she's become a yoga guru for elderly ladies and a staunch advocate of the continental workday. It's all about the "rhythms of life," apparently. My mother's theories of the rhythms of life are very attractive if you are over sixty; they don't have a whole lot to do with earning a living. They involve sleeping as much as you want, going on beach trips to the south of France, and (this with a particularly unctuous expression) devoting Real Energy to Your Family. What this seems to mean, in practice, is reproaching your eldest daughter for living three and a half thousand miles away. Of course it also means adopting a particularly pained expression whenever said daughter talks about the pressures of work, the lack of time she gets to spend with her husband, the challenges of trying to combine office-and home-life. It's really a great theory, because it means you don't have to sympathize with your eldest daughter on any of these issues, you can just tell her that her life is ideologically flawed and honestly what does she expect? And when will she see sense and come back to the land of moderation and rationality, the land where (she insists) family still comes first? After all, look at Alison…

Alison has become A-number-one daughter, her star in the ascendant as mine precipitously declined. She's a wonderful disciple of the rhythms-of-life theory, a first-class sleeper and frequenter of beach resorts, and those bottomless pots don't interfere much with life as a mummy. It turns out that my mother didn't really want us to go into the professions after all, she wanted us to marry rich men and have **them** do all the work. Wish I'd cottoned onto that one years ago, it would have saved me a lot of bother.

Anyway, today, for whatever reason, she limited the number of catty comments, and we chatted amicably about family politics. She doesn't approve of Jeanie's boyfriend, and neither do I, so this is a pretty safe topic. My horrible uncle Richard (Ma's older brother) sold his pad in Malta at a loss last week; another safe topic, since we both experience an unseemly delight at anything that makes Richard unhappy. She also told me her plans to expand the yoga business over the next year—she wants to hire a second instructor, which seems like an excellent idea, if only to facilitate those beach trips and maybe, just maybe, so she can come out here and see the baby. It's funny, in spite of her pro-family pitch, it doesn't seem to have crossed her mind to keep me company for a week or two while I'm on bed rest. Can't leave the yoga studio, she says. Now, isn't that an example of work getting in the way of family? (But did I say that on the phone just now? No, of course not. We're getting on for the moment, said the good daughter voice in my ear; don't rock the boat. Maybe you can ask her the next time. Except I know I won't. I won't have the nerve.)

1:30 P.M.

I ate the prosciutto sandwich, chips, and banana Tom left me about an hour ago, and I've been waiting hopefully for Brianna for the last twenty minutes. But it looks like—

2:45 P.M.

Well, fortunately Brianna showed up just as I was about to commit hara-kiri from hunger and boredom. There's a lot more to Brianna than I realized. Today she brought me a platter heaped with noodles and sugar snap peas from a gourmet buffet, followed by a Stollen, a bag of marzipan Kugeln from one of the German stores around the corner, **and** a selection of three excellent chocolate chip cookies (white, dark, and milk chocolate chips in crispy thin biscuit, delicately buttery with a light sugar snap).

Once again, the tax for this culinary largesse was thirty-five minutes on the subject of the Married Man. The story gets worse and worse. Married Man and Married Woman have two children, and MW has just told MM she's pregnant with the third. Brianna thinks it's all a con on the wife's part; forget the wife, I thought to myself, maybe it's MM who's doing the conning…Of course, he's had to explain how the woman he can "barely bring himself to touch" has become pregnant with his kid; he told Brianna it was just a one-night thing after the wife's father had a heart attack a few months back. Had we heard anything about MW's father's heart attack before this? Had we heard about MW's inconsolable distress and her insatiable demand for sex in the aftermath? No, we had not, but this doesn't seem to bother Brianna. She's swallowing the whole lot hook, line, maggot, and sinker. You have to hand it to him, MM is doing an excellent job here. He's found the one woman in the City of New York who hasn't heard these lines before and he's peddling them for all he's worth. Unfortunately, as Brianna gets to know me better, she's becoming less inhibited about telling me the raw details of the affair. I now know, therefore:

- that he likes her to dress up in red velvet bustiers with nipple rings, fishnet stockings, and black suspenders ("my wife gets so self-conscious");
- that his number one fantasy is for her to dress up as a hooker (a red velvet bustier-wearing hooker, you understand), and for him to drive by and pick her up;
- that she's thinking about going along with the above, but she has some serious reservations ("Q, I might get **arrested**!");

• that his wife taunts him about his flabby body and middle-aging spread, while Brianna makes him feel like a Real Man (ha!).

So I listen with the appearance of interest while Brianna tells me all of this, slurping noodles as I go. Oh, who am I kidding, I'm fascinated by her sex life at this point. **My** red velvet bustier has been lost in the back of the sock drawer for a long time now, and the last time Tom and I shared a fantasy it involved a three-bedroom house in the 'burbs with a decent-size garden and a Viking stove.

Perhaps it's not surprising, then, that I saw Brianna go back to the office with something oddly close to regret. She's not the sharpest tack in the tool drawer, but she's a helluva lot more interesting than the four walls of our small yellow sitting room.

8

Wednesday 9 A.M.

I can't bear it, I don't think I can bear it. This morning I awoke at six to the sound of the door slamming as Tom left for work, and I began to panic; fear rose like vomit in my throat, I felt as if I was about to choke. I have to get through this entire day, here, on my own—and the next, and the next, and the next, stretching on and on through the next three months (thirteen weeks, ninety-one days, two thousand one hundred and eighty-four hours, one hundred and thirty-one thousand and forty minutes—).

I'm going to lose a whole season. It's February now, I'll miss this year's spring completely. Not that it's much to write home about on the East Coast, not like in England—the daffodils will be out now in Oxford, banks of purple and yellow crocuses clustering under the trees in the Trinity gardens—but still, I'll miss that sense of the year's lightening; the first warm day, the first glimmer of green beneath the snow-killed grass in the park.

I am lonely. I am bored. I am scared. I am hungry.

10 A.M.

I'm going to learn to knit. I just looked up "wool" on the Web and found a Manhattan store that has a Web site. I ordered five balls of something called "cashmerino baby" in pale blue. Then I ordered two pairs of bamboo needles and a book called **Knitting for Novices.** I finished up the order with a funky knitting bag with matching needle case in pink and taupe stripes. Very 1950s.

10:30 A.M.

Who am I kidding? I'm not going to teach myself to knit. I can't even sew—I refused to learn at school, decided (aged six) it was a dying art, so instead I devoted my time to learning how to stick pins into the skin of my forefinger without drawing blood. I may have an alternative career as an acupuncturist, but my chances of knitting a pair of bootees for our baby seem slim. And do I really want the bootees anyway? Surely we'd prefer a few pairs of serviceable white cotton socks from the Gap?

What am I going to do—what am I going to do—what am I going to do—?

11:15 A.M.

I am going to commit myself to increasing my knowledge of black-and-white cinema. I'll draw up a list of the great movies I've always meant to watch and work my way through the genres—silent, action, film noir, foreign, documentary. I'll take notes on them to remind me of all the plots, the actors, the directors, and who won which Oscars. By the time this baby comes I'll have a compendious knowledge of Great Film—I'll be the kind of person who dashes to obscure art cinemas to watch newly discovered footage from a prewar Russian documentary. I'll slip in references to my "favorite" Japanese filmmaker at dinner parties.

I'll talk knowledgably about "cinematography." I'll be able to check the box marked "be an impressive conversationalist" on the Modern Woman's List of Things to Do Before Hitting Thirty.

11:30 A.M.

But I'm never going to go to dinner parties again, am I? And I'm not going to have the time for obscure art films either. After all, who'll look after the baby? I can hardly take him with me; highbrow cinema-goers won't think much of a screaming toddler. There's no point in educating myself in Great Film. I'm going to spend the next ten years of my life attending Disney movies filled with princesses and dancing turtles.

I have no life now, and I'll never have a life again. I might as well face the facts. My youth is over. This is simply a taste of what's to come. I'm not **me** anymore; I'm not a lawyer, I'm not Tom's lover, I'm a body, a vehicle, an incubator. I'm "a means, a stage, a cow-in-calf," as Sylvia Plath put it. My whole being is devoted to preserving another life. My own life has effectively ended. Bed rest just means it ended a little earlier than expected.

11:45 A.M.

Cut all of the above. ✂ ✂ ✂. I can't believe I was complaining about the restrictions the baby is placing on me when I don't even know if he'll

live. What kind of a mother am I? If I was any kind of a woman I wouldn't begrudge losing these last few months of my freedom. What the hell is **wrong** with me?

9

Thursday

Slept all day, watched TV.

10

Friday

Slept, watched TV, slept some more.

11

Saturday

Tom working. Watched TV. Cried. Ate cookies.

12

Sunday

Tom working **again**. Cried hysterically. Ate
cookies.

13

Monday Noon

Several important things happened this morning:

- A visit to Cherise revealed that my fluid level
  has risen slightly.
- The condo newsletter arrived under the
  door, and I discovered that my funny Greek
  lady is—how unlikely!—leading a group of
  local people opposed to the demolition of
  the apartment building opposite.

My fluid level is still too low; Dr. Weinberg
showed me a chart. But at least I'm not at the
very bottom of the chart anymore; there's a chink
of daylight now between me and impending

disaster. So maybe the bed rest is helping? I can't quite believe it, I find it hard to accept that lying on a sofa all day affects those irregularly shaped pockets of black at the baby's shoulders, hips, and toes. But who knows. The important thing is—as Dr. Weinberg told me, a smile pinned firmly to her darkly lipsticked mouth—my condition is not getting **worse**.

As regards the Greek lady, it seems she's something of a mover in local politics. Turns out that both our building and the one opposite, the one whose residents I watch when there's nothing good on the TV, are owned by the same landlord; both were populated in the 1950s and 1960s by a number of Greek and Cypriot immigrants (I always wondered why you find such good dolmades around here). Fast-forward fifty years: the complex opposite is now infested with toxic mold, the black kind, the type that embeds itself deep into the Sheetrock, breeds greedily, then takes over the atmosphere. So the landlord plans to demolish the building and replace it with something more modern and yuppie-pleasing. But the now-elderly residents have no desire to move out of their homes, and they've been fighting the development tooth and nail. I have to say, in my opinion, you don't mess with toxic mold. Just last month I read in the **Times** about some child in Queens who almost died from respiratory problems caused by the stuff, and there have been megasuits against realty companies for mold-friendly construction these last few years. Personally, I think the residents should cut their losses and hightail it out of there. Black mold is scary.

Anyway, today I feel able to take an interest in the world once again, mostly because:

- Jeanie phoned to say she's found a flight and is coming out on Thursday evening!

I'm not sure which of us is most delighted, me or Tom. He's finding me pretty difficult to deal with right now. I made him come home early on Sunday afternoon—he called around 2 P.M. to ask if I was doing a little better (he left me a weeping drooling slobbering mess at 7 A.M.) and I said, no, honestly, I'm worse. I don't think I can take this much longer. I'm going off my head with boredom and fear. After a brief, strained silence he agreed to head home, and he arrived an hour later with an armful of movies and a bottle of merlot ("Doctor Tom's orders, Q, no arguing, a glass of this and you're bound to feel better"). But he knows, and I know, that he can't slip out from the office every afternoon I'm feeling miserable. As he reminded me yet again today, the senior partners at his firm have made it clear he has to be an exemplary employee if he's going to make partner next summer. He's a fabulous lawyer, and he has a great deal of support, but Crimpson is one of the top three firms in the city, and it's promoted only a handful of its senior associates these past few years. Plus he's had the odd nasty mishap in the last twelve months. Let's just say the words "Trump" and "Donald" are rarely uttered in our home. He's got to persuade the partners he's not only capable but entirely committed to his job if he's to become a Crimpson partner himself.

Oh where oh where does that leave me...lonely and bored is where—lonely, bored, and hungry. Very hungry. Still, for the next week at least, Jeanie can look after me. I can send her out for different kinds of foods and magazines, I can make her fetch me chocolate chip cookies (the best American invention of all time, if you ask me, with lightbulbs a distant second), play games, and maybe even figure out how to knit something with my five balls of cashmerino wool (currently unopened in their padded brown envelope and stuffed under a pile of bills and unread magazines—did I really think I was going to read **The Economist**?). I'll knit myself a scarf I think, it can't be that hard. It'll be like when we were kids and we tried to carve totem poles out of sticks we found in the garden. I don't think we ever managed a recognizable totem, but we had a lot of fun trying. Alison used to get all snooty about our efforts (and she'd threaten to tell our mother that we'd taken the knives from the kitchen drawer), but Jeanie and I were undeterred. Once Jeanie got to be about eight, she was great fun. A lot more fun than Alison. It'll be fantastic to have her here for a whole week.

Horrible boyfriend is not coming along, which Jeanie is upset about—I think she was hoping to combine looking after me with a romantic touristy getaway in the Big Apple (take in a few Broadway shows, eat at some expensive trendy restaurant, waste wads of cash in Niketown, all the sorts of things my English friends seem hell-bent on doing when they come to visit). But the thought of having the horrible boyfriend in my apartment—in what's about to become my baby's nursery—filled me with dread and disgust, although I didn't say much about it (okay, so I might have mentioned that I didn't want his smelly feet stinking up the place, but they really are **rank**). Anyway, it's a dead issue because he can't get the time off work, and now that he actually **has** a job...He also can't afford the plane fare, and while I'm happy to contribute air miles to the Jeanie fund, I'm sure as hell not paying for that lousy toadstool of a man. So, horrible boyfriend will be all on his own in London, and I can spend seven days explaining to my misguided little sister why he's Not Good for Her. Perfect!

She's a funny girl, Jeanie. I've never understood why someone so attractive—she has big brown eyes, a boyish slender figure, and long, perfectly straight fair hair (so much nicer than my wispy red stuff)—is drawn to such losers. I mean, Mike Novak was a nimwit, but at least he had prospects in the medical profession, and Alison's boyfriends, while uniformly irritating, were usually at least talented, titled, or good-looking. But Jeanie has a rare talent for falling in love with men who are singularly ungifted in the looks department—the more pock marks the better—and still have an ego the size of the London Eye. It's a phenomenon peculiar to the male species, I think; show me a girl with weight problems, greasy hair, and zits and I'll show you someone who spends her life indoors hiding behind a pair of darkened spectacles and a large-brimmed hat. But you'll find a man with the same unprepossessing characteristics (and let's throw in bad breath and body odor for good measure) strutting his stuff in every club in England on a Saturday night, blithely chatting up any babe unlucky enough to come within ten feet of him and confidently telling his mates he's "in there."

Most girls, of course, tip their vodka-and-orange over said disgusting slimeball, but Jeanie is one of those weird people who decides he's "just being friendly." Dave—the charming beau of the moment—turned up in one of her evening classes (she's putting herself through a graduate program in social work), and he was, apparently, remarkably "friendly" from the get-go. In fact, his chief appeal seems to have been that, for the first month, he followed her around with the devotion of a dog (its personal hygiene habits also, I must add). The library, the pub, the bus stop—you name it, Jeanie told me, Dave was there, waiting for her with a hopeful look in his eye. I'd have called my lawyer and got a restraining order slapped on the nauseating bit of pond weed, but Jeanie thought this was all rather sweet, so she rewarded him at the end of a month by going to bed with him. Not, she admitted, that she fancied him exactly, but she thought his dogged affection proved that he really cared for her. She was not deterred by the fact that by this point he'd been chucked off the social work course for nonpayment of fees, dragged before the courts for nonpayment of the council tax, and kicked out of his job at the local café for persistently turning up late. He was just at a bad point in his life," Jeanie told me optimistically; "he really needs someone to **believe** in him."

My mother thinks Jeanie is programmed by her experiences with my father to fall for useless men, but I think it has to be more complicated than that; my father brushed his teeth and washed his hair, for god's sake, and he didn't exude Dave's air of disreputable sliminess. Tom thinks Jeanie felt deserted by my father, ignored (in favor of Alison and me) by my mother, and left out by us two older girls when we were growing up, and so she's now looking for someone to make her the center of their universe. I think that's nonsense. It's true that I enjoyed making my two sisters compete for my attention when I was a kid—which was a bit mean, I grant you, but I'm sure I'm not the first oldest child in the world to do it. And Jeanie knows I love her. If I hadn't left for New York just after Alison's marriage to the honorable Gregory Fuckwit (as I like to call him), I think we'd have become really close.

10 P.M.

Tom just called to say he'll be home in an hour. I could hear the anxiety in his breathing as soon as I picked up the phone—"Q, I can't get out yet, please don't be mad at me, okay?" But rather than yelling wrathfully at him or whispering brokenly that I need him **now,** I told him "he should take as long as he needs…"! So maybe I've turned a corner, maybe I'm sort of **adapting** to this curious new life. The pregnancy seems to be going better, Jeanie's coming here in four days, and Brianna swept in at 4 P.M. and left me with three boxes of all-butter cookies from some delicatessen in the Village.

14

Tuesday 2 P.M.

Just as I was about to devour my lunchtime smoked-ham-and-Cheshire-cheese sandwich—it was literally on its way to my mouth—there was a knock on the door and there stood Mrs. Gianopoulou (aka my funny Greek lady, aka president of Residents Against Demolition) with an absolutely extraordinary food platter. Creamy hummus, shiny purple olives, zesty dolmades, and fresh warm pita, all excellent, all homemade. I was positively moved. Funny that my two most devoted visitors since I've been on bed rest have been a girl I hardly know from the office and a woman I'd never met from my apartment complex.

Anyway, I asked Mrs. G to stay and share some of the platter with me, and after some hesitation she agreed. I'm not sure how old she is—certainly well over sixty—but she's quite a stylish-looking woman in an older-person sort of way. She wears her silvering hair pulled back in a bun, which emphasizes the strong cheekbones beneath her olive skin, and her green eyes are flecked with gold. I don't think she pays much attention to what she wears, but she has a southerner's love of color; most days she sports what my mother calls "slacks," crease-free trousers in bright pinks and oranges, topped with striped cotton shirts and cheery home-knit sweaters. She isn't thin, but she isn't fat either, more cushiony and comfortable-looking, and she has a lovely smile. Her presence in our apartment—these four too-familiar walls—feels like a breath of warm fresh air. (And she helped me tidy up the room a bit as well—it's amazing how much rubbish accumulates when you can't get out of bed to chuck things in the trash. Actually to be honest, she scuttled around the room depositing chocolate wrappers and take-out cartons into a succession of plastic bags while I lay on the sofa and chirruped thankfully at her.)

Over lunch we talked about her presidency of Residents Against Demolition. She seems to think that a few doses of Clorox and a good scrub would sort out the mold problem—and raised her right eyebrow in a distinctly skeptical fashion when I advanced my "black-mold-is-one-step-down-from-the-black-death" theory. I asked her why she's leading the residents' action group, given that she doesn't actually live in the condemned building, and she looked at me reproachfully. Then she asked what I would do if my friends were about to lose their homes. But I think she is inspired by more than mere philanthropy; she seems to feel that she's partly responsible for the landlord's decision to destroy the building because she was encouraging her friends in the complex to agitate over the quality of services he's providing. Like many of the residents in the condemned complex, she has a rent-controlled apartment, and as we all know, landlords aren't especially keen to throw money at tenants renting desirable Upper-East-Side properties at a fraction of their market value. She has apparently filed several complaints about the quality of the services she's received over the last year and helped half a dozen friends in the other building make similar complaints. She thinks the landlord was rattled by the sudden influx of grievance letters and trumped up the black mold theory in response.

She also thinks that our building is next—she believes destruction of the first complex will set a precedent somehow, and she's clearly worried about losing her home. But, as I told her, if our apartments turn out to be free of toxic mold, there's nothing the development company can do to her; as a rent-controlled tenant, she can't be evicted. It's different for Tom and me, of course; if the landlord wants to renovate our apartment we'll have to move out at the end of our lease, but we've got another twelve months to go, and by then—who knows?—maybe we'll be in our three-bedroomed house, cooking on our shiny silver Viking stove.

I always have some sympathy with landlords in this position. They're just trying to earn a living like everybody else. But if Mrs. G is to be believed, ours has been shortchanging the rent-controlled residents for years, and he has now written a shamefully high-handed letter telling them they'll have to move out within a matter of weeks and offering shockingly poor compensation. If the building has serious mold the residents will have to leave, as I explained, but of course they have rights. Mrs. G and her friends are unsure how to respond; Mrs. G's great-nephew, Alexis, has been helping them translate the landlord's various communications, but he has admitted that he doesn't understand the landlord's latest statement of the case and of his legal responsibilities.

So I offered—oh lord!—to look at this latest document and try to explain it to Alexis and Mrs. G. I tried extremely hard to make her understand that I was **not** going to act as their lawyer in all of this, but I'm not entirely sure she got it; I told her they needed to hire a lawyer officially to represent their interests, but she looked extremely blank and said "You not lawyer, then?" with big round eyes. She's going to ask Alexis to drop by one night this week after school (he's a history teacher) and bring the letter, and I'll have to tell him that my advice is strictly off the record. I really don't think I can get involved in this; even if the residents were able to pay me, I can't function effectively as a lawyer while lying on my left side twenty-four hours a day. And Dr. Weinberg would have a **fit** if she found out.

Am I being played by old Mrs. G? Maybe. Maybe I'm going to seriously regret offering to help, but I don't see what else I can do. Mrs. G has been like a mother to me this past week—not like **my** mother, obviously, more like the mother I always wished I had. She makes me things to eat, she listens to me sympathetically when I'm upset, and other than that she **leaves me alone**. This is pretty much perfect mother behavior, as far as I'm concerned. The least I can do is explain the contents of a letter to her.

Today, for the first time, she also told me a bit about her own life. She was engaged thirty-five years ago to a man who was blown up in Vietnam a week before he was due to return home for the wedding. And that, as far as she was concerned, was that. "In my mind, we married, you know?" she said to me, her eyes suddenly bright. "Still married. There can be nobody else. He was everything. My sister in Philadelphia, she's so cross with me, thinks I've ruined my life, but I'm happy, you know? Happy as I can be without **him**. Alexis looks after me, I see my friends, I go out, I have good life. Don't know why people make me do what everybody else does, move on like nothing happened. When you find the right person, that's it, you joined up forever. Know what I mean?"

I nodded slowly. What would happen if Tom— no, no, it doesn't bear thinking about. But my mother was kind of like Mrs. G, she rarely dated again after my father walked out, although I don't think it was because she felt "joined up forever." I think she just thought life was too short to waste on any more rat-bags.

7 P.M.

Disaster! Brianna's married lover dumped her last night!

They went out for drinks, she expected the usual amorous relations to ensue, but he coldly gave her her congé halfway through a large dry martini. And what, as she said, do you do after that? Draw out the painful breakup as you delicately sip the remainder of your spirits or down the thing in one hasty gulp, risking swollen numb lips and stripped cheek cells? In the end she decided on the old-fashioned alternative (I always said she was a 1950s girl) and splashed the entire contents of the glass in his eyeballs. And then (because what was he to do with **his** drink? she pondered, being a thoughtful girl in her way), she picked up her lover's glass, dipstick, olive, and all, and dumped it down the back of his neck as she marched out of the bar.

She called me a few hours ago and asked if she could come round. I must admit, I was intrigued to find out more about this unexpected breakup. Why did MM leave his extraordinarily gullible and willing mistress? Was it the impending arrival of a new baby—**or** was it Brianna's discomfort at the idea of parading the streets of Manhattan in suspenders and a crimson velvet corset?

MM, with typical skill and aplomb, managed to make Brianna feel responsible for the disastrous finale. I suspect that the wife got suspicious, because apparently Brianna broke rule number one of the relationship by calling his cell phone a few days ago, thereby leaving an unfamiliar number in the last ten calls. **And** as MM had often pointed out, the wife was likely to check through the numbers. Brianna also made the mistake, I gather, of insisting that MM spend a weekend away with her sometime in the next month, and further suggested that he might like to leave his wife now, rather than in five months' time, when the wife is on the verge of delivering a screaming nine-pounder. In other words, she became just a teensy bit more demanding, a weensy bit less submissive, and MM took to his heels in a fright.

Of course, Brianna is now racked with guilt ("I pushed him too hard...of course the pregnancy must have shocked him...of course he can't leave his wife while she's suffering from morning sickness...of course I should have worn the bustier..."). I stroked her shoulder and said "there there" a lot, and watched someone else work their way through the box of pink tissues I keep on the teak side table. It was quite nice not to be the one weeping for a change. I told her she deserved better, that she was a beautiful and intelligent (?) girl and should date men who appreciated her finer qualities. She sobbed brokenly, then pulled herself together, smiled mistily at me, and said I was probably right. She thanked me for listening and consoling her in her hour of need, and told me I was very wise. I felt wonderfully maternal. ("Give wise advice to friends in need" is another item on the Modern Woman's List of Things to Do Before Hitting Thirty.)

Tom called a few minutes ago to say he's on his way home for dinner, so Brianna decided to go home, have a bath, and work her way through a vat of chocolate fudge ice cream (my idea). I think I've calmed her down. In fact, I think she's starting to see she's well rid of the bastard.

10:30 P.M.

Tom tells me he bumped into Mark in the subway on the way home. Apparently, Lara is pregnant again! Seems everyone's up the duff these days.

15

Wednesday 9 A.M.

Jeanie is coming tomorrow—I can't wait. Only thirty-three hours to go before she lands.

10 A.M.

Just had Brianna on the phone. Last night's tub of ice cream and my dose of measured advice only accomplished so much, it seems. She woke up in floods of tears (she told me), sobbed all the way to work, and now wanted my approval of her plan to go home and wallow in misery under the bedcovers for the rest of the day. I said, **No!** Absolutely not. No wallowing allowed. Chocolate consumption is one thing; wallowing under the comforter is quite another. Stay at your desk, I admonished her firmly, but you can come and see me at lunchtime and we'll share a box of cookies, if you like.

2 P.M.

I've just posted her back to the office. She wanted to spend the rest of the day here ("we can keep each other company"), but I was having none of it. I mean, I like her, and I feel sorry for her, but

I have my own problems. And anyway, she has to start getting over this. It would be one thing if her married lover had a single redeeming feature, but he doesn't; he cheats on his wife and kids, he's an unusually harsh lawyer (Brianna concedes—he's apparently got the social conscience of a mole rat), and he's a master in the art of manipulating weedy needy girls. What's to like?

4 P.M.

Another hour-long call from Brianna. I'm utterly worn out.

6 P.M.

The doorbell rang a few minutes ago. It was Brianna; I could hear her heavy breaths through the door. I'm ashamed to say this, but I pretended to be asleep.

6:10 P.M.

Brianna just called on her cell and asked if I was okay, telling me she was worried when I didn't answer the bell...I trotted out the line about having been asleep, silently cursing myself for having picked up the phone. She asked if she could come by; she sounded so broken and distraught I felt I had to say yes. At least she offered to bring four pints of Ben & Jerry's super-fudge-chunk ice cream. With a jar of chocolate sauce.

Midnight

Tom has just kicked out Brianna. He'd been staring at her with an increasingly outraged expression on his face for the last two hours, as she oscillated interminably between extolling MM's virtues (he was "caring," which translated means that he bought her a turquoise bracelet from Tiffany's for her last birthday) and cataloging his physical faults (his wife had a point about his middle-aging body, she now admits; his tummy is charging outward while his hairline is in full retreat). Huge yawns didn't seem to register with her, neither did the fact that at one point I actually fell asleep in the conversation (a misnomer if ever there was one; she talked, we listened in silence, eyelids propped open with matchsticks). Finally Tom stood up and said courteously but firmly—every inch the practiced, polished lawyer—that **I** needed my rest and **he** had an early start at work tomorrow morning. She looked a bit taken aback, but Tom adroitly maneuvered her off the armchair and out of the door before she had the chance to ask—and I knew it was coming—if she could crash in our spare room tonight. Jeanie in my baby's room, yes; all others, most definitely **No**.

16

Thursday 7 A.M.

I didn't sleep last night—maybe I'm still preoccupied with Brianna's crisis, maybe I'm overexcited about Jeanie's arrival this evening. Either way, my night was filled with strange hallucinogenic dreams; at one point I woke up with warm sweat pooled along my spine, convinced I'd given birth to triplets with kittens' heads.

And my legs are starting to protest their new purposelessness. The tendons whine, the bones groan, the joints flatly refuse to cooperate when I roll and twist my ankles to try and force the blood into my freezing toes. And then there's the cramp, that unexpected nighttime horror of pregnancy. I catch myself clinging to consciousness because my body knows that, in sleep, I may point my toes down and start up a pain that is surely as bad or worse than birth itself. (Or if it isn't, somebody let me off this train.)

8 A.M.

Bri just called **again**. She tells me that she's going to stay at home all day and cry, unless I can give her a reason to get up. Really, truly, I can't.

After five minutes I pretended I had to go to the bathroom. So sorry, Bri.

10:30 A.M.

Jeanie will be at her gate in Heathrow now. The plane will probably be boarding. I hope she's remembered to buy a spare bottle of water for the journey, I **did** tell her.

Noon

Jeanie's plane has taken off—I've been following its progress on the Virgin Atlantic Web site. It looks like she's going to arrive on time. In about seven hours she will walk through our door.

Brianna on the phone once more, so I used the "I have to pee" line again. It's going to get old, but what can I do? I can't be "on my way out the door" or "in the middle of cooking dinner" while I'm on bed rest, and I simply can't—no, no, **no**—listen to any more on the subject of the MM. I feel trapped. When Jeanie gets here I'll have to tell her to start screening my calls.

Midnight

Jeanie and I have been talking nonstop for the last five hours—about everything: the pregnancy, Alison, our mother, the studio, her course—

everything. It's so good to see her. It's almost worth being on bed rest to have her here with me at last.

17

Sunday 4 P.M.

Best things about having Jeanie here:

- She is an **excellent** cook, and I was longing for some homemade food. (We've eaten takeout every night since the first day I was placed on bed rest. Manhattan may have the world's best restaurants, but there's only so much saturated fat a girl can take.) Last night we had spinach lasagne, the evening before we had duck casserole, and she made a big pot of apple and parsnip soup for lunch today. She's promised to make more and leave it in the freezer before she goes, together with some whole-grain rolls. Yum.
- She's the one member of my family Tom actually likes.
- I have a reason to fob off Brianna whenever she calls ("Sorry! Jeanie's calling me, must put down the phone…").

(Poor Bri, I think she feels I've abandoned her now that Jeanie's here—which, in all honesty, I have. But after a few Brifree, tear-free days I'm ready to face her again, so I've asked her to come over on Tuesday at seven to meet Jeanie. Hopefully my sister's presence will force her to keep a lid on things a bit, and anyway she can only stay for an hour because the MM has asked her to meet him for drinks to "talk things over.")

Worst things about having Jeanie here:

- Turns out she already knew how to knit. Not sure I like the fact that my youngest sister is more accomplished in the feminine arts than I am. She's already a much better cook. ("Become competent in the feminine arts" is another item on the Modern Woman's List of Things to Do Before Hitting Thirty. I want my children to grow up in a household where larders are stocked with luminous homemade jellies and rich amber chutneys in sparkling glass jars.)
- I'm sleeping terribly and am **longing** for a night alone in bed, but Jeanie's in the spare room so I can't kick Tom out.
- Jeanie calls Dave at least once a day and croons lovingly at him until I want to vomit.

18

Tuesday 9 P.M.

Jeanie's gone to have drinks with a school friend who recently moved to Brooklyn, so I have a few minutes to write up the events of this evening—

At six-thirty the doorbell went, and I thought, Christ, Brianna has come early so she can spend an extra half hour droning on about the MM. But no—it was Mrs. Gianopoulou accompanied by Alexis, her great-nephew (I'd completely forgotten they were going to drop in with the latest letter from the landlord).

First things first: Alexis seemed extremely nice, the kind of person you'd love to have teaching your ten-year-old. He looks a bit like Noah Wyle—well, like Noah Wyle would look if he'd had a Greek grandmother. He has clear, shy eyes, sun-brown skin, and floppy golden hair, and he was dressed very stylishly for a high school teacher, in Diesel jeans and a Paul Smith shirt. I bet all his pupils have enormous crushes on him. (I almost have a crush on him myself, except it's hard to lust after strange men when you can barely see them over the top of your belly.)

He gave me the letter, which I soon realized he understood far better than Mrs. Gianopoulou thought. In fact, he was painfully uncomfortable

about asking my advice; he understood immediately that I wasn't acting as their lawyer, and
when Mrs. G went out of the room to use the
bathroom he admitted he's been trying to persuade the group for months to raise the money to
hire their own representation, officially. But the
older residents are unwilling to part with their
cash (to be fair, they don't have much), and they
don't see why Alexis can't handle the landlord all
on his own.

Alexis, perched on the edge of our leather
armchair, ran his fingers through his hair with an
air of deep, lifelong exasperation. "Don't get me
wrong, I'm happy to help out, y'know?" he said.
"But as far as the old people are concerned, with
a good American education I should be able to
take on the whole Randalls corporation, save everybody's homes, and guarantee them all a happy, peaceful retirement. I try to point out it's not
as easy as that—I don't have any legal training,
I'm just using my common sense—but they act
like I'm somehow trying to screw them around.
I know this isn't fair to you, but if you can read
the letter and give me some pointers, tell me what
you think—I'd really appreciate it."

Poor man, I thought. What a responsibility. (He uncrossed his legs at that moment and I
caught myself staring covertly at the bulge in his
black jeans, but then the baby kicked reproachfully. My tiny hormone surge subsided limply.)

I sighed and skimmed the letter quickly. It explained that Randalls had hired Environment First, a private environmental inspection firm, to assess the mold in December of last year. Randalls included a summary of the report with their letter. Environment First found evidence of **Stachybotrys atra** (black mold) together with **Aspergillus ustus** and **Penicillium fungi** throughout the building. Apparently there has been a series of catastrophic water leaks over the last ten years, which caused the initial mold infestations; many of the construction materials used back in the 1940s—ceiling tiles and so forth—are cellulose-based, and this has left the complex particularly susceptible to mold growth. Virtually none of the apartments are mold-free, and those on the ground floor (the site of a burst water pipe about two years ago) are particularly affected. The cost of a cleanup would almost certainly outweigh the cost of destroying the complex and building a new one, so Environment First "recommends immediate evacuation of the apartments and their subsequent demolition" (the line from the report was quoted in the letter in bold fourteen-point type).

In light of this, the letter from Randalls concludes, leases will not be renewed and tenants are required to vacate within ninety days of the expiration of their lease term. Each household will be paid a reasonable sum in relocation expenses, and appropriate alternative accommodation will be provided in another Randalls-owned building. Yours faithfully, Coleman and Elgin Randall.

Together with Environment First's statement was a fuzzy Xerox of a note from the New York State Division of Housing and Community Renewal acknowledging Randalls' application to demolish the building.

I read all of this and shook my head sadly. Given the rising costs of litigation on the part of residents who want restitution for the health costs of living in a building with mold, it's hard to blame a property owner who takes his environmental responsibilities so seriously, I thought. The residents are screwed, I thought. If the building has to be demolished, it has to be demolished. There's nothing I or anyone else can do, although I can probably recommend a lawyer who will make sure the tenants are getting reasonable compensation.

But then I paused; some wormy wriggly idea was trying to force its way into the forefront of my consciousness. Something was missing. This is not my area of law, but—where was the order **approving** the application to demolish? I stared solemnly into the depths of the brown envelope from Randalls; I read the letter again, looking for a reference, a passing comment. Nothing. I chewed my pen contemplatively while Alexis stared at me hopefully. Environment First is a private inspection company, and private companies don't have the authority to enforce demolition. In order to destroy a building inhabited by residents **in rent-controlled apartments,** Randalls has to provide all tenants with a copy of a notice from the Division of Housing approving the demolition.

It was so simple, so straightforward, that I paused a moment longer. Then I asked Alexis if he'd seen an official statement of condemnation at any point in the process, and he told me he hadn't; at that moment Mrs. G reappeared from the bathroom, and he asked her in Greek if she'd heard anything about it. She shrugged her shoulders, pulled down the corners of her mouth, and said, no, never. Well, I said, it may not hold off the demolition forever, but they can't kick out your friends without the DHCR's approval notice. Maybe it already exists, maybe Randalls simply forgot to include it with this letter, but still, without it, you can seriously hold things up.

"By the way, I don't suppose you remember the name of Randalls' lawyers, do you?" I asked; Alexis shook his head, then looked over at Mrs. G, who wrinkled her nose. "I think—we had a letter once from Smith and—someone, and the Smith was spelt funny, you know?" she said uncertainly. I nodded. "Smyth and Westlon, I know them," I said. "They do a lot of eviction stuff. Fine, send them a copy of your letter as well, Alexis, that should help."

Alexis, I noticed, had developed a tight, anxious expression. "So you want me to write to both

Randalls and the lawyers, asking them where this approval notice from the—DC—the DH—the whoever it is, is? What was the name of it again—wait, I must find a pen…then maybe you can tell me what to say to all these guys…"

I watched him scrabble in the pocket of his jacket, thrown over the back of the armchair, for a moment or two. Mrs. G watched me watch him. Her expression was pregnant with meaning. I sighed.

"Alexis, don't worry about it, okay?" I said, gently. "I'll write it all down for you. In fact, I'll draft a letter stating that the residents won't leave until they've received copies of the official notice, then you can adapt it however you want, give it to Mrs. G, and she can sign it. And I'll get you Smyth and Westlon's address as well. Okay?"

"Oh, that's be **great,**" said Alexis delightedly, his face becomingly flushed with relief. He reached for my hand and shook it warmly; Mrs. G gave me an approving nod. As they got up to leave, the doorbell rang. This time, it was Brianna, who bumped into Alexis in the doorway, then did a double-take, blushed, looked down, and pushed a loose strand of dark hair away from her ear, exposing her throat, the side of her peach-skin neck. The pheromones were still tingling in the air half an hour after she left.

19

Wednesday 4 P.M.

We just got back from the doctor's office—Jeanie took me this week, so Tom could put in more hours at work. He's helping finalize the details on a huge, $300 million bid for some Midtown office space (Crimpson has one of the biggest real estate departments in the city). The weather is utterly miserable; it's one of those days where the clouds squat down on the sidewalks, enveloping everything in a dripping dirty gray mist.

First of all Cherise, the ash-blond technician, did her usual thing. I watched the baby on the monitor for a few moments, then lay back and looked around the gloomy examining room. Cherise has placed things above the couch that are clearly supposed to keep patients of all ages and both genders entertained—a mobile of three cartoonish chickens in a chain, four black-and-white postcards of Harley-Davidson motorcycles, and a page of "Dos and Don'ts" from **Marie Claire** (avoid strapless tops if you have rounded shoulders, halter tops make small busts look bigger, long-waisted shirts help conceal a large tummy. Nothing about hiding double chins and puffy ankles, I noticed).

After ten minutes of prodding and rubbing and pushing Cherise told me flatly—it had to happen—that my fluid level has now dropped.

Weinberg was consulting a book entitled **High-Risk Pregnancies and Their Outcomes** when I entered her room; she smiled brightly, too brightly, as she slid **High-Risk Pregnancies** discreetly under the latest copy of **The Jewish Week**.

"I want you to come in on Friday for something called a 'nonstress test,'" she said, very cheerfully. "A nonstress test checks the strength and regularity of a baby's heartbeat; it's no big deal. It's just a precaution. I'm sure everything's fine. But—tell me," she added, her tone studiedly casual, "has your little one been active this past week? Are his kicks still strong?"

Of course I knew what she was saying. Is he healthy, will he survive? Truthfully, I don't know if this is "an active little one" or not. Some days I get kicks so hard they leave me breathless, other days I feel almost nothing, just a tiny catch in my pelvis, the merest flicker under my ribs. What does that mean?

I'm worried that my fluid dropped because—if I'm going to be completely honest—I've been up and about more since Jeanie arrived. Yes, I make her fill up my water jug and fetch me breakfast and lunch, but I couldn't resist the temptation to take her on a little walk of our block the first day she arrived. She tried to prevent me, of course, but I played the "I'm your older sister and I know what I'm doing" card. And it was an unusually warm day, the last of the slushy snow melting in the light of a clear blue sky. So now I feel guilty, worried that my ten-minute perambulation of the local bars, restaurants, and fruiteries has put our baby's life at risk. (I haven't told Tom about the walk yet, and it's been weighing heavily on my conscience—I'm going to have to admit it tonight, when I tell him the result of today's investigations. He can be rather frightening when he gets angry, he turns on this ghastly lawyer-in-a-courtroom thing that I've never quite mastered. "I present you with exhibit A, an empty toilet roll. Can you explain, please, how it is that this empty toilet roll was not replaced with exhibit B, the full toilet roll, which resides in the bathroom cabinet, as shown on map C? Well?")

Jeanie had obviously decided before she came that the whole bed rest thing was ridiculous; the trip to Weinberg's office today seems to have changed her mind. On the telephone a week or two ago she said to me, cheerily, "You know what I think, Q? In another era you wouldn't have known a thing about this oligo-whatever-it-is and you'd have produced a completely healthy child in three months' time." But in the sonographer's office today, as we watched the baby hunched into something that looked like the Little Ease torture chamber in the Tower of London, she felt for my hand. I caught sight of the stricken look on her face. "It says on the screen that the baby's head is in the twentieth percentile," she whispered to me at one point, uncertainly. "Is that okay?"

She's off tomorrow, and I'm nervous at the thought of being alone again day in, day out. But I'm not **entirely** sad that she's going. I don't want to have to hold things together for her any more—I want **her** to reassure **me,** not the other way around. After we got home she kept saying positive things that were on the verge of making me feel better when she would spoil the effect entirely by turning them into questions. "I think the doctor's pretty optimistic about your condition—isn't she?" she said, gazing at my belly with an anxious eye. "I know the baby's a bit small, but size doesn't mean anything—or does it?" And then, falteringly, "Everything's going to be okay, right, Q? Right?" That's the problem with being the older kid. You always have to be the grown-up in these situations. I smiled brightly at her. Of course everything's going to be okay, I said firmly. Of course.

The other upside of Jeanie's departure: I'm longing to send Tom into the spare room so that I can have the bed to myself. My eyes are red-rimmed, the skin on my face seems to be stretched in one unending yawn. My legs ache, my hips ache, my knees ache, my back aches, my head aches. I want to sleep for a thousand years.

20

Friday 10 A.M.

Jeanie left at four o'clock yesterday afternoon for JFK. In the evening I dispatched Tom into the spare room, turned our double bed into a pregnant-woman-comfort-zone (pillows at every limb), and settled down to enjoy a long night of uninterrupted sleep.

But that's not what happened. True, Tom's absence meant I could finally throw open the windows and enjoy the subzero temperatures of a New York night in February (my pregnant body seems to think it's in a Guatemalan heat wave), but I **still** couldn't sleep. The pressure pain along my left side remains close to unendurable. Taxis, drunken men, and street cleaners seem to conspire to keep me in a state of constant near-consciousness. Every twenty minutes I need to guzzle a barrel of water to quench my Saharan thirst. Whenever sleep seems beguilingly within my grasp, I either have to pee, or an ambulance screams frantically past, and I'm jolted back into hot, aching, heavy-lidded wakefulness.

So I spent much of last night staring at our lavender-painted bedroom walls—or rather, watching the gray give way to purple with the dawn—just as I have watched this same slow battle of colors every night these last few interminable weeks.

Tom, at least, looked a bit more human this morning; he's been positively skeletal these last few weeks, his blue-green eyes ringed with black. "Well, Q, that was an improvement," he said cheerily as he grabbed his navy coat and scarf from the closet. "I actually got some sleep without you kicking about. We may just have to sleep apart for the remainder of your pregnancy," he added, barely a shade less cheery, dropping a light kiss on my clammy forehead. "At least that way we'll go into parenthood well rested," he finished, with a positively sunny smile on his face as he picked up his heavy maroon leather briefcase and vanished into the corridor, leaving a smell of burnt toast and marmalade hanging thickly in the air behind him.

I lay staring at the closed door for a long time after he left. I, of course, continue to look like one of the Undead, but my husband didn't seem to notice. He didn't make **me** a slice of toast and marmalade this morning ("Sorry, honey, didn't realize you were awake, I thought you'd be sleeping in." As if). He also forgot, for the first time since the first day of bed rest, to make me a sandwich for lunch and snacks (i.e., cookies, cake, brownies) for the day. And finally, he didn't mention—I don't know if he's even remembered—that he is supposed to take me to the clinic this afternoon for the nonstress test. One night apart, and already he's slipped the leash. He's become **one of them,** a "normal" person who gets up in the morning and goes to work, an ordinary guy leading an ordinary life. Meanwhile I lie here hour after hour, nothing to separate morning from afternoon, weekday from weekend. I've never felt so alone.

Tom's gone, and Jeanie's gone, and I'm alone. Alone with the memory of the stupid, horrible argument I had with Jeanie just before she left for the airport yesterday afternoon. It was the old argument, the one we've been having for the last twenty years, dressed up in adult clothes. She asked me to come and spend a week with her and Dave in a Cornwall cottage this autumn, and I made it perfectly clear that I wouldn't set foot in a house that contained him. She became increasingly upset and said, but you'll go to stay with Alison even though you hate Greg, so why won't you take a holiday with me and Dave? And I said, because Greg at least washes himself and doesn't pick his nose in front of the television—but it's not worth recording what I said, because what

I was really trying to do was hurt her. I watched the stricken expression in her eyes, I watched the corners of her mouth quiver, and suddenly she was seven years old all over again, and I was twelve, and we were playing outside at our home in Kent…

—Jeanie following me around the rose-filled garden—Jeanie wanting my attention—Jeanie asking me to come and play with her—and instead I take Alison's arm in mine and lead her off to read teenage magazines under the bramble bushes that edge the field. I see the appalled expression in my littlest sister's eyes, and I feel a delighted sense of power, I realize that I can make someone else feel the way **I** feel when my mother looks at me with vacant eyes—"you're too young, you're just a baby, you can't play with us big kids"—"I'm sorry, Q, I have more important things to do, someone has to earn a living around here, go and play on your own, or can't you entertain yourself yet? Dearie me, what a **very** little girl you are still, you have a lot of growing up to do…"

Well, now Jeanie has gone, and I am faced with the prospect of the next ten weeks on my own, day and night. Serves me right.

I should call Tom to remind him about the appointment. But perhaps I won't. Perhaps I will order a taxi to take me to the clinic instead. That'll serve him. He'll feel really guilty this evening, when I tell him I struggled to Dr. Weinberg's office on my own, blinking in the daylight, a heavy pregnant woman with dwindling muscle tone.

Noon

Okay, scrub all of the above. Self-indulgent non-sense. I highlighted it and was about to hit the scissors icon, but then my compulsive need to record **all** my thoughts in this diary stopped me from doing it. Anyway, Tom just called; he's coming to pick me up in ten minutes. He remembered the appointment in plenty of time, and he's promised to bring a prosciutto and artichoke-heart sub with him for my lunch. **And** a chocolate chip cookie.

7 P.M.

I'm typing this in a hospital bed.

Tom has just dashed out the door to get me some dinner. By my side, on a small laminate table, reposes the meal the hospital provided at five-thirty, which looks entirely inedible. A viscous meat loaf oozes into stringy green beans; also provided is soup of indeterminate vegetables, a browning banana, and a cellophane-wrapped cookie (at least they got one thing right). Tom and I stared at each other over the rapidly congealing meat loaf for a while, then we decided to resist the entropy that seemed to be closing in on us. Food, at least, we can control. A large pizza with tomato and basil and a fresh Caesar salad should be here in about fifteen minutes.

It's funny that the thing we had this afternoon is called a "nonstress test." It was the most stressful test I've taken in my life.

It started out reasonably enough. I hoisted myself onto the examining couch in the sonographer's office, and—I know the drill—pulled up my shirt to expose my belly. Cherise covered me with the usual dollop of translucent blue goo, then settled herself into her chair and checked the baby's position and my fluid level, which was the same as the other day. Fine, I thought. This won't take too long. I'll be out of here in half an hour.

After that, she secured two round discs to my stomach with elastic belts; one (pink belt) measured the baby's heartbeat, the other (blue belt) checked to see if I was having contractions. Then she gave me a plastic cupful of orange juice to give the baby a sugar rush, and told me to settle down and wait. I examined the "Dos and Don'ts" page again on the ceiling above the couch: Do team tailored pants with broderie anglaise shirts for a look that's both professional and feminine. Don't wear beaded sweater-tops if you're a busty gal.

The sound of the baby's heartbeat filled the room. A backdrop of swooshes punctuated by regular lilting thuds; **lub-dup, lup-dup, lup-dup**. A number flickered green on the monitor:

139, 142, 143, 145. The normally po-faced Cherise flashed a sudden, unexpected smile. That's a good reading, she conceded; the baby's heartrate sounds strong. Now we'll record what happens when he kicks in response to the sugar. Dr. Weinberg wants to see a varied heartrate, it's the sign of a healthy baby. I'll be back in ten minutes to check up on you, she finished, and disappeared into the corridor. The large door banged shut behind her.

Tom and I, hands clasped tightly in the warm semidarkness, watched the screen and the heart's gentle rise and fall. 135, 132, 138, 142. Tom tapped his foot in time to the rhythm ("This is quite fun, Q, don't know what you were so worried about"). After just a few minutes, I felt the baby begin to kick lustily, saw the tiny bulges in my stomach forced by a flailing hand or foot, and a demisecond later the beats soared to 150, 155, 160, 165. "Great, looks like we're done here, why don't you go and tell Cherise," I told Tom, intensely relieved. He nodded and went off into the corridor to find her.

Except that, seconds after he left the room, something started to happen. Swooosh, swoooosh, **lub—dup; lub——dup...lub——dup**; the gaps between the thuds are growing, the swooshes sound like a river of slowing treacle. And the number on the screen is dropping fast—120, 118, 104, 97, 92—

—and now I'm panicking, the number's dropping like a stone, and I'm calling for Tom while frantically massaging my belly, and the tiny hard body curled beneath my tightly stretched skin. I don't know what I thought the massaging would do, but I wanted to make contact with my little one, to tell him I'm here, and hang on, please! Hang on!

Tom heard the sound of the slowing heartbeat out in the corridor and rushed in with a white-green face, the technician a pace or two behind him. She took one look at the monitor, then barked at me: "turn onto your side, NOW! We have to move this baby off his cord." I couldn't think what she was talking about, but I hastily turned over, and as I did so the monitor went silent, and it was the loudest, most ominous silence I've ever heard. I heard myself wailing "what does that mean? Is he dead?" Cherise slipped the discs all over my stomach as I flopped about like a freshly caught fish, trying somehow to restart his heart (as I imagined) while she slithered the discs across the surface of my belly—until, "Hold still!" she said finally, urgently; "**he isn't dead,** the disc has just slipped off his heart and we've lost the signal, you've got to stay still while I try to find it"—and then suddenly we heard it again, loud and strong and clear this time, 130, 135, 137, 135. The green numbers blinked reassuringly at us.

Tom collapsed into a plastic chair and buried his head in his hands; I was shaking violently. Cherise took a deep breath. "Stay on your side for now, okay?" she ordered: "Everything's probably fine, but I'm going to get Weinberg just in case. I'll be back in a minute or two."

After a minute's bewildered wait Dr. Weinberg came in, smiled briefly at us, then examined the long stretch of red-lined graph paper spewing out of the monitor. A crazy line measured the peaks and troughs of the baby's heart rate; I could see that one long dip, ending in blankness. I stared at her, willing her to tell me that this is normal, that they see this all the time—

Except of course, that's not what she told us. She sat on the side of the examining couch and took my hand; I held on tight, like I was drowning. "Listen to me, **mein bubeleh,**" she said, gently. "I think the baby is getting into difficulty, I think he's constricting his umbilical cord when he moves. Amniotic fluid is a sort of cushion between the baby and its cord, and you don't have enough, **versteh**? The drop in heart rate tells me he's not getting enough oxygen. I've got to send you into the hospital."

So here we are. I'm lying in a narrow bed hooked up to an IV, typing on my electronic organizer (which I found half an hour ago in the depths of my handbag, thank God, somewhere between a mashed-up tube of Tums and a scattering of lidless pens. Tom's promised to bring my computer in tomorrow). In the corner of the room a monitor blinks. 130, 132, 145, 140.

21

Saturday 2 A.M.

I've had twenty minutes' sleep so far tonight.

Just as I began to lose consciousness a few minutes ago, a nurse named Andrea came in to check my vitals. **Blood pressure, pulse, temperature, and are you in any pain? Describe your pain on a scale of one to ten...** I swear, when I get out of this place, I will stop complaining about bed rest. I will never complain about the lack of sleep again. I will never complain about lying on my left side again. I didn't know how good I had it until today. Hospitals **really suck**.

I am terrified of the monitor. I can't stop staring at it. Every time the green number starts to drop in the darkness I turn rigid with fear.

3 A.M.

The baby's heart rate just plummeted. I noticed the slowdown (**lub——dup; lub——dup**) and pushed my call button in a panic; Andrea appeared and told me, in soothing tones, not to worry, she was keeping an eye on my monitor from her nursing station. "It's not a great reading, but it's not terrible either," she said, a hint of Irish in her voice; she swears she'll come in and help me move into a new position, one that moves the baby off his umbilical cord, if the heart rate drops dangerously. But Andrea seems seriously overstretched to me. What happens when she's helping the woman with triplets in room 027? I have turned up the volume on the monitor, despite Andrea's entreaties, so that I can check on him without having to twist around in my bed to face the screen. I'm his mother, I must keep him safe.

22

Saturday 4 A.M.

In the darkness I listen to his heartbeat. **Lub-dup. Lub-dup. Lub-dup**.

In the darkness **he** listens to **my** heartbeat. **Lub-dup. Lub-dup. Lup-dup**.

23

10 A.M.

Less than twenty-four hours ago I was at home. Thirty-six hours ago Jeanie was here. Unbelievable. I seem to have been in this hospital for about a century. My life has shrunk to this one small room, to a narrow metal bed and a bleeping monitor, to a heavy, stretched white belly.

They brought me my breakfast at around eight, and I must be losing my mind because I fell upon the rubbery omelet and the cardboard carton of ultra-high-pasteurized milk with absolute glee. I polished off the entire contents of the tray in about five minutes. I am a very hungry pregnant woman, this is my only excuse.

Just as I was licking the last morsel of cold home-fried potato off my fork, a young resident with a round shaved head came in and examined the monitor printout. He shrugged. This isn't bad at all, he told me; only one period of deceleration, and the baby's heart picked up again fairly quickly. This is actually very reassuring. We may be able to discharge you in the next few days, he said casually as he vanished out the door to attend to the woman with triplets in 027.

I was left staring after him with my mouth open. All night I've been imagining horrors—

death, neurological damage, permanent disabilities—and now someone tells me the baby may be fine after all! Relieved, I called Tom to pass on the good news; he told me he's organizing things so he can take an hour off this afternoon to spend with me. He was very pleased with himself for thinking of it ("it's not easy to arrange, Q, but I've explained to Phil, the senior partner I'm working with on this bid, that it's very important"). I can't help reflecting that it's the least he can do. Partner Shmartner, I want someone holding my hand.

11:30 A.M.

Ten minutes ago someone calling himself "the attending" bustled in. Before I knew what was happening, my knees were gaping at the ceiling and a strange man was fiddling about down there with something that looked (and felt) like a pointy silver fork. After five extremely uncomfortable, not to say awkward, minutes, the strange man snapped off his vaguely sexual latex gloves and told me flatly that he was "not yet reassured" about the baby's condition. Unlike the cheery resident, he agrees with Dr. Weinberg that the baby may be squishing his cord in periods of activity, and he wants to go on with continuous monitoring. Before leaving he produced an ominous leaflet about steroid treatment from the right-hand pocket of his officious white coat.

"If we think the baby isn't thriving inside we're going to induce labor, despite the fact that your child's lungs are unlikely to be mature," he told me, neutrally. "Steroids will fast-track lung development and give him a better chance of survival, but he will need to be admitted to the intensive care unit for the first few weeks." (This with all the emotion of one indicating the need for some moderately serious toenail treatment.)

He left me in a state of confusion. I'm bewildered by the different views of my condition; everyone seems to have their own opinion about how my baby is doing. Frankly, I'm increasingly convinced that no one knows what the hell is going on in there. Why do I have this problem? ("There are lots of possible reasons," the attending told me judiciously. "But, truthfully, we have no idea.") Will my son be healthy? ("We don't know the answer to that one either," he admitted.) What's wrong with my uterus? Will it happen again? ("Ask another," he said as he backed sheepishly out the door.)

He did tell me that my son will be a little under three pounds if he has to be delivered this week. That's less than my laptop.

I have to stay calm.

Tom still isn't here, goddamn it, so in desperation I called my mother. This, of course, was a mistake.

"Jeanie told me about that walk you took," she said, viciously. "Q, I despair of you, really I do. One day you will stop putting yourself first! One day you will learn about the kinds of sacrifices parents make for their children..."

Enough is enough, I thought as her voice droned on in my ear. So what sacrifices have you made for **me**? I cut in, bitterly. When did you put me first, precisely? When I was six, and you told me I couldn't have a birthday party because you were too busy preparing for a meeting with the bank's examiners? Or when I was ten, and you canceled my ballet classes because you were tired of driving across town to the studio? Or perhaps when I was fifteen, when you forgot to come and see me perform in the final heat of the national poetry-reading competition and blamed your secretary for failing to remind you?

I made all sorts of sacrifices for you, she said, in astonished fury, and I only had one diary and my secretary was in charge of it. Of course it was her fault I missed the competition, you don't think I wanted to, do you? I can't believe you're **still** bringing that up! And what was I supposed to do about the ballet classes, three kids all wanting different things, if it wasn't ballet it was the trombone or the bloody triangle, I couldn't get to them all, and your wretched father never learned to drive...

Christ, I yelled down the phone, don't give me that, you found the time to turn in sixteen-hour days at the office, you could have driven me fifteen minutes to ballet lessons! Dad may not have been able to drive, but at least he was home to give us a bath at night! The day you told me I couldn't have a birthday party he threw me one all by himself, dressed up as a clown and served me green jelly and ice cream with cupcakes. I've never forgotten that, it's one of my happiest childhood memories. I don't think you star in any of **those,** let me tell you—

And then I stopped, because things were getting out of hand. I couldn't quite believe what I'd just said, and I don't think she could either. There was a long silence.

"June Whitfield's daughter says that your hospital has an excellent obstetrics unit and a fantastic neonatal intensive-care facility," she said, suddenly and unexpectedly. "World famous, apparently," she went on, with a tiny catch in the back of her throat. "It's quite a relief, really, knowing you're getting such good care, Q!"

I can't quite express how surprising I found this statement. Apart from the fact that I thought she was about to disinherit me, I never expected to hear my mother describe a New York institution as anything other than (a) corrupt or (b) incompetent. I paused.

Five minutes later, I discovered us in the middle of a perfectly amicable conversation about my baby, my treatment, and June Whitfield's daughter's hysterectomy. For some reason, my mother backed down this time, God alone knows why. Could it be that, just this one time, she decided not to fight with me because of my circumstances? Could it be that she was putting me and my needs **first**?

Midnight

Tom has just left. In the end he wasn't able to take an hour off this afternoon (at the last minute he was told to redraft a clause on the property bid, so he told me), but he did arrive at my bedside at ten-thirty with my laptop and three large brown shopping bags piled high with junk food—pizza, fries, cola, cookies, cake. "Sorry, Q," he called as he ran into the room, half out of breath; "but this lot's bound to make you feel better! I ran round the market on the corner and got a trolley full of real crap. Not a vitamin in sight." I appreciate the thought, although now, after three and a half thousand calories of fat and carbohydrates, I feel sick. And I need to pee, but I can't face the hassle of unhooking myself from the monitor and dragging myself and my IV across the chilly floor to the bathroom. Plus I get nervous that something will happen while I'm off the monitor, that my baby's heart will slow down, and I **won't know**.

24

Sunday 4 A.M.

I've just had a nightmare. I dreamed I was in the hospital, in serious danger of delivering my baby two and a half months early. I woke up, and for a few groggy moments I thought, it's okay Q, it was just a nightmare, you're safe at home! Then I heard the sounds of muted activity in the corridor, saw the bright white light shining under the metal doorjamb, felt the IV needle sharp in my wrist and the plastic discs bound tight to my abdomen, and I realized with a dawning sensation of misery that it was all **true**.

7 A.M.

I feel disgusting. I haven't showered in two days. My hair feels thick and greasy, my face is sticky, and I'm longing to wear something that doesn't have a slit down the back. Plus I haven't been able to take my bra off since Friday because I can't get it over the IV stand. I tried last night, managed to get it off my shoulders, over the IV tube and the water bag, all the way to the top of the support stand and then right down to the bottom, but no matter how hard I tried I couldn't get it over the stand's four metal feet. The elastic stubbornly refused to stretch. So there I was, crouched and groveling on the tiled bathroom floor, bra-less, with my hospital shirt round my ankles, hoping desperately that the nurse (Eddie) would **not** choose that moment to check on my blood pressure.

The good news, though, is that the baby hasn't had any real problems; his heart rate dropped a little bit at about 5 A.M., but mostly he's stayed up in (what Eddie likes to call) "the comfort zone."

8 A.M.

Today's "attending" has just visited, and told me I can take a shower this morning.

She checked the monitor printouts and seemed quite pleased with the results. She told me that Dr. Weinberg was worried the baby's heart rate was dropping regularly, to lower and lower speeds, and so far the hospital's tests seem to prove that, in fact, it isn't. This suggests he's not damaging his umbilical cord too seriously when he moves—occasional lapses are tolerable, it seems—so on the whole they've decided they are (that word again) "reassured."

I'm very relieved, although the attending said it's still possible they'll keep me in the hospital for the remainder of the pregnancy. Then, if the baby gets into trouble, they'll be able to act quickly. Apparently there's going to be a meeting to discuss this possibility at 10 A.M. this morning. I'm torn between feeling rather important (a whole meeting about **me**! Lots of doctors in white coats talking about **me**!) and annoyed at this irritating race of people with God complexes having a meeting about me without me there. And Tom too, of course.

About ten minutes after the attending doctor left, Dr. Weinberg called on the telephone. Will I carry this baby to term? I asked her. (The hospital medics may have found reassurance, but I'm still searching for it myself.) To term?—oy **oy oy**, I doubt it, she said, with a heavy exhalation that crackled the line. I'll be pleased if you make thirty-five weeks. The way things are going now your fluid will run out, and then your little one will do better outside you, in an incubator if necessary. But he may be able to breathe unassisted, and you'll certainly be able to breast-feed him, by thirty-five weeks. So let's shoot for that, okay?

So this is my new goal. Five more weeks—thirty-five days, eight hundred and forty hours. It's not so much. Even if I have to stay in here, attached to a monitor, it's not so much.

All at once, the baby feels real to me in a way he never has before, not even when I watched him, tiny legs paddling, on Cherise's ultrasound screen. My ears are filled with the sound of his existence, his alive-ness. We lie here companionably together, listening to each other's heartbeat. *Love set you going like a fat gold watch,* I told him. That's Sylvia Plath. I'll tell you all about her, one day.

His heart rate is comfortably up at the moment; I feel I can risk unhooking myself from the monitor to get into the shower.

9 A.M.

I am clean, I am new. I have never been so pure.

That's Plath again, although I think in her case it was inspired by something other than a bottle of kiwi-and-lime shampoo and a free sachet of peaches-and-cream conditioner found (by Eddie) under the counter of a nursing station. After slathering myself with these excessively scented unguents I feel like a completely different woman (although I fear I smell like a large fruit salad). I moisturized my face, dried my hair, put on black mascara (why not), and slipped on a clean hospital gown. Okay, so it still has a slit up the back and a cutesy floral print, but at least it has starched creases and a complete lack of tomato ketchup stains (it's hard to eat home fries in bed). And

I've rid myself of that pesky bra at last; my newly rounded maternal breasts jiggle about under my gown like two baby seals in a sack.

My little boy is clearly feeling the effects of the last chocolate chip cookie because he is kicking and squirming; my stomach undulates with each movement. He must like cookies as much as his mother.

4 P.M.

Tom has just left.

He was here for about forty minutes, then he received a phone call from one of the partners asking him to go back to the office immediately. I watched him talking into the phone ("Really? Can't—? No, I see. Okay. But really—okay. Yes. Okay.") and I knew that something was up, that something was wrong; his eyes kept flicking toward me, then uncomfortably flicking away. At the end of the conversation he snapped his silver phone shut, still without meeting my gaze, then told me that he may have to go to Tucson in a few weeks' time to work with one of Crimpson's biggest clients on a series of new hotel leases.

I gasped. **Tucson?** If they send me home, how will I cope on my own? And if I'm still in the hospital, how will I pass the days without him?

I couldn't quite believe what he was suggesting. Dimly I heard him saying something about how his mother could come and take care of me ("I know it's not ideal, Q, but she wants to be more involved in our lives, this might be a real opportunity...") and I blenched; **Lucille** of all people, my God, was he serious? I stared up at him for a few moments without speaking. Then I told him to try and get out of the Tucson trip. And before I knew what I was saying I was asking if he **really** has to make partner at his firm, or if he'd consider switching jobs to a smaller, less prestigious firm, one that actually lets you go home for the weekend and eat dinner with your kids.

He was standing by the end of the bed, fiddling with the tip of his silk striped tie the way he always does when he's stressed. As my words sank in, he glanced over at me for a second or two, and in his eyes I saw many things: distress, anger, disappointment, frustration—many things. He looked away again before I had time to determine which feeling was uppermost. He has the most wonderful eyes—blue-green, sea-colored, and the sudden sight of them made me remember all over again that I love him (so much). But even as I remembered, words seemed to be tumbling out of my mouth, whitewater words crashing into the air, explaining that something has changed, that from now on I want to feel he's putting me **first**. And when this all ends, after we have the baby, I'm going to want to feel the same way.

I'm sick of never seeing you, I told him, carried away on a wave of emotion. I'm sick of having food thrown at me as you vanish out the door— I'm your wife, not a sea lion, what am I supposed to do, gulp down the fish and clap my hands? I'm sick of packing our relationship into fifteen minutes in the morning and fifteen minutes at night. I want our weekends back, I want them like they used to be, the first months we were together. I want to get lost in Central Park. I want to get sunburned on Jones Beach. I want to drink dangerously large martinis then feel each other up through the seven languorously served courses of dinner at L'Espinasse.

After a minute or two he turned and walked away from the end of the bed and went to stand by the window. I watched him watch the Manhattan afternoon pass by. The noise of the traffic is muted by the thick hospital glazing; inside, I feel shielded from the busy world outside. I'm still and quiet, lying here, while it rushes loudly past. Until now, I've only thought about how oppressive the silence and the stillness are, how depressing, how boring. But today I realize I actually like the feeling of being quietly cocooned in here with the baby. Of course I get scared, and bored, but I like not having to organize my life into increments of time, into fifteen-minute billable blocks listed in an oppressively large black leather desk diary. And I want him to share something of this with me. I want to spend at least part of these long irksome days breathing in time with him, learning again to read his thoughts.

Tom listened to me tell him this with his face half-hidden in the lengthening shadows of a raw March afternoon. He has spent very little time in the hospital with me, and he admitted suddenly that this has been deliberate. He has found worrying about me and thinking about me incredibly tiring this past month, he said, his voice strained and thin. The knowledge that I'm fed and provided for in a hospital has been a relief, he added, and as he turned around to face the bed I saw the dog-tired expression on his face. "I'm sorry, Q, I know this is hard on you," he went on. "But Christ, it's hard on **me,** getting up and going to work, doing all the usual stuff, and making sure you're provided for as well. As for Crimson—Q, listen to me, I've wanted this job for **ten years**. I'm trying to make partner at one of the biggest and most important firms in the city. I'm working to achieve my life's biggest ambition. Don't tell me to quit, honey, please…"

I stared at him. An ice cube seemed to be melting, slowly, in the pit of my stomach. Suddenly he slumped on the bed beside me, reached out, and took my hand. "Q, I love you," he said, earnestly, to my fingers. "I love you **so much,** you know that. But we knew it was going to be hard when we decided to have a baby, right? We agreed we'd make it work somehow, right? And that's all I'm asking now, for us to do what we said we'd do, a few months ago..."

Mark and Lara called five minutes ago to tell me they are coming to visit this evening. I can't stand them, but at least they'll help me keep my mind off all this.

8 P.M.

Something extraordinary has happened.

It's about Mark and Lara, and—

Wait, I'm going to tell the story in the order in which things happened.

Mark and Lara arrived at 6 P.M. Lara looked impossibly elegant in a monochromatic Chanel pantsuit. The creases in my floral hospital gown wilted at the mere sight of her.

"I'm sure you know I'm pregnant," she said, settling into the nursing glider beside my bed and kicking off her barely-pink suede kitten-heeled boots. "I'm three months' gone," she added, with an oh-so-casual glance down at her oh-so-flat, couture-encased belly. I caught the self-satisfied expression in her eye. By her stage I was already confined to elastic-waisted nylon skirts from Target.

"Yes, I heard," I said sourly. (What's this? I thought. Go-wind-up-the-high-risk-pregnant-woman-in-hospital day?)

"Of course," she went on, swinging her legs off the glider footrest and affecting a look of earnest importance, "the timing is bad. It's difficult for us to celebrate, obviously."

I was a bit taken aback. "You needn't feel that my condition—er—should prevent **you**—er," I began, awkwardly.

Lara trilled with laughter. "Oh no, Q," she said, cheerfully. "I don't mean **you**! I mean"—pause to refix expression of earnest importance on her face—"my **father**. He's still very ill, you know. Yes, it's a trying time for my family. Being in this hospital—well, it brings back the whole ordeal, to be honest. I think I shall have my baby at a birthing center; I can't deal with hospital karma, not after what I've been through…"

As she wittered on about birthing suites, doulas, and so forth, somewhere in the back of my brain something stirred. With an effort I managed to pin down a memory of a late-night phone call a few months ago, in which Mark asked Tom if he could recommend a heart specialist (Tom's father is a surgeon at Johns Hopkins). Lara's father had just had a heart attack, and Mark was trying to do something useful to help out.

"It's been an appalling shock for me," I heard her say. "I've been on antidepressants since my mother called with the news. But my doctor says they won't have any effect on the baby, and the most important thing is for me to find peace. And

I think that's right, don't you? I can't be a good mother unless I'm at one with myself…"

Mark was standing where Tom stood earlier this afternoon, by the window, staring out at the Manhattan streets. I could see the faint balding spot on the back of his head, the pink skin showing through his coarse, sparse hair. Tom claims that Mark used to be very good-looking; I can hardly believe it, we're not that old yet, surely, he's only a few years past thirty—

It was already quite dark outside. Loops of white lights threaded through the trees sparkled along the busy sidewalks, illuminating the crowds of people attending to their infinitely varied concerns.

Lara was still talking.

"Although if we're going to be honest—just between us girls—I wouldn't be having this baby if it wasn't for my father's illness. So there is definitely a silver lining to this cloud. You must know what I mean!" she said, with a hideous simper.

I blinked. "Sorry?" I said, baffled. "I don't think I do—"

Mark was still standing silently, hands plunged deep into the side pockets of his blue jeans. He didn't seem to be paying attention to our conversation. Lara glanced at his back, then leaned in toward me.

"I mean the baby was conceived **that night,**" she murmured in my ear, with an arch, conspiratorial smile. "The night of my father's heart attack. Quite a night it was too—I didn't think Mark could make me forget something so awful, but he was so, well, **demanding,** it was— mmmmm—just **thrilling**…"

And she began to whisper all sorts of things about their sexual goings-on the night her father was taken ill, about Mark's long-standing fantasy for her to don a red velvet bustier and walk the nighttime streets, and her sudden capitulation…

Her final words sunk in a few seconds after she'd uttered them. **A red velvet**—good God!… "Yes," Lara continued, mistaking my choking gasp, "I know what you mean, I don't mind admitting I found the whole thing rather **slutty,** but my brush with death left me feeling so **reckless,** and really, Q, it was the most incredible sex I've ever had, Mark put on quite a performance—"

"Lara, for God's sake!" Mark broke in; he'd clearly just realized the turn the conversation had taken. He pulled his hands out of his pockets and planted them firmly on his hips. "What the hell are you talking about?" he asked, with a dark, furious expression on his face.

Lara laughed her arch laugh again, then stretched back languorously in the glider. "Oh, **baby,** you needn't be so shy, I'm doing you justice after all!" she said, slipping (I'm not making this up) her little finger into her mouth and biting

the nail in what I imagine she took to be a devilishly sexy fashion.

Mark folded his arms tightly across his chest.
"I don't think Q is interested in hearing about
our sex life, Lara, and it embarrasses the hell out
of me, so let's change the subject, okay?" he said,
his body rigid with irritation. Lara shrugged and
threw me an amused look. I studiously avoided
her eye.

They left about ten minutes later, but I don't
remember a word of what we talked about. Sentences were playing and replaying in my mind,
sentences which on first hearing seemed simply
clichéd but have now acquired the unmistakable
sheen of truth: "my wife's on antidepressants…"
"she's so self-conscious…" "her father's heart attack…" "I can't leave because of the children…"
And that red velvet corset, the cause of poor Brianna's torment—

Because surely—**Mark is Brianna's MM!**
They must have met at work, when Brianna was a
paralegal in the Manhattan Assistant U.S. Attorney's office. I'd never quite put it together before,
but they certainly must have worked in the same
office at the same time—and Brianna **did** tell me
her lover was a lawyer with a distinct lack of social
conscience…

If I'm right, I bet Mark has broken off the relationship not just because of the pregnancy, but

also because Lara has been taking a new view of his sexy little fantasies these past few months. Poor Brianna must have looked pretty tame beside a resplendent Lara in velvet and sables. What man wants a mistress who's more sexually reserved than his wife?

So how to proceed? Should I call Brianna and tell her what I've discovered? Should I confront Mark? Or should I tell Lara? Scrub the last option, I have no intention of exposing Mark and Brianna to Lara. Brianna because we're friends, Mark because I can't find it in my heart to blame him for running around on that flat-bellied, tight-assed daughter of Satan. It's ironic really; I thought Brianna was the world's dumbest mistress for swallowing lines like "my wife doesn't understand me," but as it turns out—I'm sure it's true!

Tom's been telling me for years that Mark's obsessive pursuit of poverty-stricken unfortunates with two grams of crack in their jeans pocket was weirdly out of character. As a law student at NYU, he was extremely active in the Human Rights Clinic; his metamorphosis into a hardnosed AUSA only took place after his marriage to Lara. Mark's ambition used to be to move back to his hometown in rural California, set up his own law firm, and provide legal representation to poor residents, on a barter system if necessary, but Lara was having none of it. She wouldn't consider moving out of Manhattan, and anyway she has precious little sympathy for the drug-embroiled ("They should learn to exercise, that's how **I** get high"). Over the years Mark seemed to take her lead, although Tom always said there was something suspiciously self-hating about his transformation into the kind of person he once despised.

Tom can be very perceptive about people.

Tom—Tom. I haven't thought about him in nearly three hours. I've been feeling secretly delighted at the problems in Lara and Mark's marriage, feeling (if I'm honest) rather smug because **my** husband isn't running around behind my back, and now it strikes me that, in a sense, he **is**. He might as well be having an affair with another woman for all the time and attention he has for me these days. His work comes first, it seems, before me, before the baby.

25

Monday 3 A.M.

Achingly tired but can't sleep. I've been thinking a lot about Tom and our conversation this afternoon. Maybe I'm not being fair. It's true we knew we were taking on a lot when we decided to try for a baby; I always understood that Tom was fiercely ambitious. It's one of the first things I loved about him, actually. He told me he wanted to make partner at Crimpson the day we met, four years ago, on a warm Sunday afternoon in early fall (the kind of afternoon that lingers long in your memory, when the heat of the pavements creeps up your knees like a lion's lick while a polar bear's breath steals through your hair). He does **try** to join me for supper, even if he has to go back to the office afterward. He gives me as much time as he has, what more can I ask?

And I know he thinks about me, and worries about me, all the time. A taut, set look settles over his face whenever he sees me trying to keep myself occupied with nothing but a laptop, a few dog-eared magazines, and a plate of food. "I wish I could do this for you," he said to me once, his voice low, stifled. "I wish I could carry the baby instead of you." And he tries to think of treats to raise my spirits: one evening, when he couldn't make it home before bedtime, he arranged for a courier to bring me a bunch of gigantic Asiatic lilies, delicate white and golden stars with bright red stamen. Another time he sent a box filled with cocoa-thick brownie wedges; "sweets for my sweet" he wrote in his crabbed lawyer's handwriting on the card.

Men like him don't come along all the time, they really don't.

3:30 A.M.

But there are the practicalities to consider. We're going to have a child. Am I supposed to deal with our baby on my own if he wakes up crying in the middle of the night and Tom's still working?

4 A.M.

I'm getting ahead of myself; there **is** a perfectly practical solution. I'll be on maternity leave at the very beginning, so it's only fair if I deal with the baby when he's a newborn. Then we'll get child care for the daytime, and the baby should be sleeping at nights by the time I go back to work. It'll be fine.

It's going to be a question of compromise, of balancing Tom's needs with mine. (Isn't that what the magazines and talk shows always tell us? Compromise and communicate, then everything will work out.) I'll tell him he has to eat with our son in the evenings, and after that, I'll let him do his own thing.

4:15 A.M.

Who am I kidding—according to my friends, sleeping through the night is the holy grail of parenting. The child may be a year old before I'm getting a good night's rest. Unless Tom cuts back his hours and takes his fair share of nighttime duties when I go back to work at Schuster, I'll walk blearily under the street sweeper one morning on my way to the office and that'll be an end to it all.

As for the supper thing, that'll only work if our toddler likes his spaghetti hoops at midnight. Tom **says** he'll be home in half an hour, but then he bumps into Phil or Ed or Ian, and three hours pass by. That's just the reality of our lives. Plus I don't see how **I'm** going to make partner if I end up doing 90 percent of the child care. Schuster isn't as crazy as Crimpson—it isn't as high octane, nor as elite—but if you start really trying to cut back your hours, if you get onto what Brianna heard Fay contemptuously call the "mommy track," you'll find yourself unaccountably assigned to the firm's most boring, Byzantine cases. If I'm going to be a success at Schuster, if I'm going to get real job satisfaction, I'll need to work close to as hard as I did before I went on bed rest.

Only one of the women partners at my firm has kids, and she has a full-time nanny. Take her kids to soccer practice? Forget it. She orders them a cab.

4:30 A.M.

The truth is, neither of us have the right kind of lives for parenthood. We don't have the time to raise a child. What in God's name were we thinking? Why did we get ourselves into this? Were we just frightened into it by that long, terrifying article Tom's mother sent us about the consequences of delaying conception? Was it the fact that I was starting to get choked up every time I passed a baby store (those teeny tiny onesies...)? Or was it the general, inchoate feeling that if you're married and nearly thirty, it must be time?

But now I'm starting to think we should have waited. Given our lives, our commitments, our ambitions, how on earth are we going to parent a child?

26

3 P.M.

It's a bright sunny day today; the sky is clear, cloudless, endlessly blue. Lying here, staring at the world through a triply glazed window, you could almost imagine it's summer—until you see the thin, stripped trees along the street, the pallid fawn sunshine, the pedestrians muffled up in furry coats and downy jackets. But still, there **is** something of spring in the sky today—the blue is deeper, more intense, than it was when I first went on bed rest, last month, in February.

A nurse called Jamala just told me that, because there have been no serious heart decelerations in the past twenty-four hours, the doctors have decided to discharge me after all. I'll be monitored as an outpatient for the rest of the pregnancy.

I don't know if I'm relieved or not. I'm still scared that something will go wrong and I won't know about it. On the other hand I feel dangerously on the verge of delivery in here. As long as I'm lying in a narrow hospital bed I'm a problem they want to solve; consultants watch me, speculatively, debating by the hour whether **now** is the time to induce labor, to get the baby out, to intervene. When I was about six we a had cat named Mirror who vanished early one summer morning; a few days later I found her curled up in a dark place in the garage, a litter of tortoiseshell kittens mewling beneath her swollen pink stomach. I think I feel like Mirror must have felt; I want to get away from everyone, to find a quiet place, and make a nest about me for my child.

Because whether this is the right time to have a baby or not, I want him so badly. I long to hold him, to feel the weight of him, warm, in my arms.

Over lunch I reread my diary entries for last night; I was really wound up, stomach coiled tight with fear and frustration. "Things always look worse in the hour before dawn," Mummy used to tell me when I was up late with a particularly bad bout of adolescent angst. But this wasn't just a nighttime fantasy, a horror of the darkness; Tom and I have some serious talking to do when I get out of here. The gap between us—let's face it—is getting **bigger**.

4 P.M.

The baby is kicking particularly hard at the moment, as if he's trying to let me know he's okay. And he had a long bout of hiccups a few moments ago which—my new best friend Jamala told me, with a comfortable smile as she plumped up my plastic-coated pillow—is an excellent sign of "fetal well-being." The attending told me as she signed off on me that although they expect the baby will come early, they are feeling increasingly optimistic about his health. So I feel a lot more comfortable—in fact, I've even allowed Jamala to turn off the monitor. The silence expands to fill the room. Warmed by the sun, it is deeply peaceful.

9 P.M.

I'm writing this from my own Liberty print couch, under my own blue-and-gray blanket, in my own yellow sitting room, behind my own apartment door. I am unlikely to move from here for the next five weeks. But at least I'm home.

27

Tuesday Noon

Mrs. Gianopoulou came to visit this morning, bringing spicy sausage, red pepper spread, and homemade bread for my lunch. The fragrance of the freshly baked bread is filling the apartment as I type, mixing gloriously with the fresh sunny air streaming in from the open window opposite my sofa.

As soon as Mrs. G walked through the door I remembered the letter I'm supposed to be writing to Randalls about the apartment complex opposite. Shit. The crisis over the weekend threw the whole thing completely from my mind. Mrs. G waved her hand dismissively when I began to apologize for forgetting. Please, please, she said. No problems. Baby first. But I promised her I'd draft it this afternoon, and we agreed that she and Alexis will drop in to read it tomorrow evening. Great, I thought, at least I'm getting some eye candy out of this. I wonder if he'll wear those tight black jeans again.

Brianna phoned and apologized for failing to visit me in the hospital (I **did** wonder what had happened to her, she's normally so devoted). It turns out that her grandmother was taken ill, and she's been visiting the old lady in Westchester County for the last three days. I think the time away from the city has done her good. She seems much calmer, much more balanced about Mark—or "the MM," as we continue to call him (I haven't let on yet that I know his identity), although Bri's equanimity about Mark's desertion may be caused by the advent of a new passion for Alexis. She asked me—casually—how often "that incredibly hot neighbor of yours" comes to visit. Actually, I said, he'll be here tomorrow evening to look at a letter I'm drafting for him and his aunt. Oh really, she said. Yes really, I said. Uh-**huh**, she said, in pregnant tones.

Alison also called half an hour ago to say that she may come to visit; I'll believe it when I see it, since she told me in the next breath that Gregory is up for promotion and is cozying up to his boss. They're off for a golfing weekend with "Alan and Sue" in a few weeks, and Alison is hosting an intimate little dinner party for them at the flat in Pimlico (catered by Fortnums) this weekend. I can't see her backing out of the full-court press on Alan "I'm connected to a duke by marriage" Atkins anytime soon. I met him once at one of Alison's exhibitions and found him utterly loathsome; he's typical of a certain sort of London banker, public-school educated, fat, florid, and he leans in too close when he talks to young women. Sue also seems pressed from a familiar mold: thin and angular, she has graying frizzy hair, a twittery way of speaking, and an unaccountable middle-class penchant for Laura Ashley that has survived the transition to serious wealth. Greg is on course to become Alan in about twenty years, but Alison—thank God—is unlikely to morph into Sue. Mind you, I wonder what that says about their prospects for marital success.

3 P.M.

Fay has been here! Quite extraordinary. She actually took time off to come and visit me for lunch, bringing—and I thought this was quite imaginative of her—a loaf of sourdough bread and three pots of "artisanal" preserves from Balducci's ("La famille Honoré Saint-Juste has fashioned preserves of the highest quality for six generations…every berry is personally inspected by Hubert Honoré Saint-Juste, the last of the Haute Provences Saint-Justes…"). I've already worked my way through half the jar of **cerises noirs,** and I'm well on the way through the **miel noisette.**

The most extraordinary part of this extraordinary visit was that Fay—reserved, tight-lipped Fay—unbosomed herself of her romantic travails. Her ex-girlfriend, Julia, has just moved back to the city after several years of working as a camerawoman on a sitcom in Los Angeles, and clearly assumes that their amour will recommence. Fay admitted in a startling burst of candor that it has taken her most of the last two years to recover from the breakup, and she is in no hurry to return to the arms of a woman who, however winsome, makes no bones about the fact that she'll hightail it back to L.A. if and when a new job presents itself.

It's strange how people feel they can confide in a woman on bed rest. Brianna, Lara, Fay, even Mrs. G to some extent seem to enjoy heart-to-hearts with a bed-bound Q. Maybe they think I have nothing better to do; maybe a pregnant woman in dark seclusion stirs ancient memories of wise women and mystic seers.

I am, as it happens, feeling particularly wise today. Halfway through Fay's account of Julia's iniquities it struck me that Paola, a school friend of Tom's, recently broke up with **her** girlfriend, and would make a perfect match for Fay. They both love opera (not that I realized this about Fay before today, but she just told me that she has tickets to see La Forze del Something at the Met on Saturday). **And** they both have Persian cats (yuck) **and** they recently traveled to Peru. We have a pot thrown by some Andean artisan on our windowsill, sent by Paola, so I skillfully directed Fay's attention to it, casually referred to Paola, and mentioned that she'd hiked the Inca trail to Machu Picchu last summer. Fay's eyes lit up; she's just itching to discuss the flora and fauna of the Amazon with someone, I can tell.

I assumed a suitably oracular expression and hinted that Paola might be visiting us in the next week or two. It may be time to have a party. I shall preside in a queenly fashion from my couch. "Throw fabulous parties" and "unite lonely, single friends" are **definitely** two boxes to check on the Modern Woman's List of Things to Do Before Hitting Thirty.

28

Wednesday 8:30 A.M.

I woke up at 3 A.M. in a vast, sweaty panic. I have just realized something. I'm going to have a baby in five weeks' time. Not ten weeks, like most women, but five. And I don't have a bed for the baby to sleep in. I don't have a seat for the baby to bounce in. I don't even have—wait, what else do babies need? What do they wear to bed, for example? I have no idea. And what about playtime—do newborns really need those hideous brightly colored mats my friends' children sprawl on, like tiny upended beetles? Will I be starving my child of sensory experience if I don't have Lamaze clutch cubes ready to go on the day of delivery?

I proudly refused all offers of something called a "shower" when I first found out I was pregnant. Not English, I said, cowing my American friends and colleagues into silence with an airy wave of the hand; not English **at all**.

This may have been a mistake.

9 A.M.

I have consulted the Web. Babyfocus.com provides a list of all the things you need as a new parent. They divide necessities up into different categories. I can barely remember all the categories, let alone the things **in** all the categories. But anyway, the salient point is this: we do not have **any** of the things in **any** of the categories. Nada. Nil. Zip. Zero. Time, Q, to swing into action. I can't go out to shop, but this is the twenty-first century, a brave new world: I have everything I need at my fingertips. I can buy things over the Web and have them delivered to our door, and very soon I will be prepared, materially at least, for motherhood.

10 A.M.

At a different point in my life, I would be overwhelmed right now. I would be baffled by the differences between a bassinet, a Moses basket, a cradle, a cot, and a crib (and life isn't made any easier by the fact that most of these things have different names in England). I would be panicked by the intricacies of mattress design and the responsibility of fending off that dreaded specter, SIDS. I would be befuddled by the range of strollers on the market, not to mention the significance of locked and unlocked front wheels and three- versus five-point harnesses. But I do not have time to be overwhelmed, baffled, or befuddled, and I am therefore responding to the bewildering array of baby "necessities" with coolness and aplomb.

I'm going to take this a step at a time. I'll concentrate on one category a day. Today's babyfocus category will be "diapering" (or nappies, as we like to call them in England, a much more friendly term I think. "Nappy" makes me think of soft, white, nubbly jersey. "Diaper" sounds like something more properly found in a toolbox). Whatever else you buy or don't buy, diapers/nappies are imperative, so this seems like a good place to start.

1 P.M.

But "diapering" turns out to have hidden complexities.

I spent an hour browsing changing tables in multiple designs and from multiple vendors before I discovered that you can buy chests of drawers with a "changing station" on top. This seems like a good idea, particularly in a small Upper-East-Side apartment. So I spent the next hour searching chests of drawers with changing table-tops, only to discover that you can also buy cribs with chests of drawers **and** changing tables built in as well. So now I'm searching cribs in addition to chests of drawers and changing tables, and my categories are getting all mixed up, and I'm on Friday's and Saturday's searches already and it's only Wednesday, and I'm all in a lather because cribs need to have all sorts of safety features, and I don't know if the all-in-one options are as safety conscious as the stand-alone ones, and all I really wanted to buy today was a bumper box of Huggies and a tube of skin cream...

And the bumper box of Huggies isn't the breezy decision I thought it would be either, because they come in all sorts of different sizes and quality ranges, and do I really need Huggies anyway? Am I being suckered into buying an expensive brand when generics are just as good? And as for the skin cream, do I want to purchase diaper rash lotion or a prophylactic ointment, and while I'm at it, do I want to take advantage of the special two-for-one deal at pharmacyusa.org and buy a tube of lanolin for nipple soreness? But "nursing" is next Monday's category, and right now I have no idea what lanolin is or whether it's something I need. I'm exhausted. Once upon a time, preparing for a baby meant sewing a few cotton nighties and fishing the family cradle out of the attic. Life is so much more complicated these days. At this speed I'll barely be ready by the time my son is born. Good thing I'm on bed rest, I suppose.

29

Thursday 7 P.M.

Diapering contd.

- 1 pack newborn diapers, 1 pack Stage One diapers ☑
- 1 Diaper Sprite diaper pail ☑
- 4 Diaper Sprite diaper pail refills ☑
- 4 packs baby wipes, unfragranced ☑
- 2 tubes vitamin A&D lotion ☑
- 1 tub diaper rash ointment ☑
- 1 changing pad, contoured ☑
- 4 changing pad covers (navy blue, stretch terry cloth) ☑
- 1 changing table/storage chest combo with canvas organizer drawers ☑

TOTAL COST: $304.98

30

Friday 8:15 P.M.

Alexis and Mrs. G have just been here to read the letter I drafted to Randalls. I am bathed in the warm glow of their gratitude. I may be barely equipped for motherhood, but at least I can write a letter to put the fear of God in Genghis Khan. Alexis smiled at me from under his dark golden floppy fringe with admiration in his eyes; Mrs. G looked maternally proud of me. Honestly, I don't know which delighted me the most.

Brianna was a no-show, which surprised me— I wonder if she's relapsed into thoughts of Mark? I hope not. She's an idiot if she passes up Alexis. He may be a few inches shorter than me, but if I wasn't a married woman with a child poking out of her abdomen, I'd be eating sun-ripened strawberries out of his belly button by now.

31

Monday 9 A.M.

I've just been checking the status of my packages, and according to fedex.com, by Wednesday afternoon I will be in possession of:

- 1 bassinet with "soothing vibrations" and a rotating musical mobile ☑
- 1 crib plus 4 cotton sheets, 1 fairground-themed bumper, and 3 matching blankets ☑
- 1 nursing glider ☑
- 1 nursing glider footrest ☑
  ($45 extra but what the hell)
- 1 changing table/chest ☑

The diapering stuff may arrive as early as tomorrow morning.

I'm starting to get my life under control.

I phoned a series of friends last night and invited them to a party on Friday evening. I could tell people were surprised to hear from me.

"Really? Oh—ah—so you're allowed to get up again, are you? I haven't been calling because I thought you were, y'know, out of circulation, and all that." This was from Patty, a fellow expat Brit, who used to be my gym buddy. She's a cousin of one of my best friends from university and moved here about two years ago to work for a publishing company.

I explained, a hint of arctic chill in my voice, that no, I wasn't allowed up yet, but that my condition didn't stop me from seeing people in the apartment. As it turns out, life is **really very boring** stuck on your left side 24/7. Some company would be welcome. This weekend. At eight o'clock. Prompt.

Oh, ah, yes, said Patty. Right. Friday night at eight it is, then.

In fact, almost everyone I phoned agreed to come after hearing my brief speech on the lonesomeness of bed rest. Guilt can be a useful thing. (My mother trained me well.)

Paola is coming up from New Jersey and will stay with a friend, and Fay has agreed to take a few hours off work to come to the party, so the pieces of that little plan are falling into place. I'll have the two of them in the same room at the same time, and with a few choice references to the mysteries of the Inca kingdom, I'll surely have them in the same bed by the end of the weekend. I've also decided that, while I'm playing Cupid, I might as well unite Brianna with the lovely Alexis. However, there's one slight problem: Tom wants to invite Mark and Lara on Friday evening as well ("Can't have a party and leave Mark out, Q, you know that"). Initially I balked, but then it struck me that the sight of Mark with Lara will surely make Brianna all the more likely to put the moves on Alexis. She'll be so desperate to prove that she's not pining away, she'll almost certainly leap into the arms of the first willing man in her path. I haven't looked forward to a party this much since my first-ever disco, at Little Stonham Village Hall, in 1985.

10 A.M.

There will be an unexpected guest at my party. I've just had another phone call from Alison.

"Q darling, I promised I'd come to help you out while you're on bed rest, and help you out I shall," she said, with an infuriating air of self-conscious self-sacrifice. "Of course, the children will miss me. Gregory will miss me. And, yes, I will miss a reception for 'women sculptors of life' hosted by the Arts Council. But My Sister Comes First. I've just bought a ticket to New York, Q; I land Friday lunchtime."

She was somewhat dismayed to hear about the party and hinted that I might like to cancel it, but she backed down when I suggested some of the things she might like to do to herself if she thought I was going to cancel my first social engagement in four and a half weeks. "No really, Q, how delightful," she said at last, through gritted teeth. "I'm very much looking forward to meeting—ah—Mike and Laura and—er—Bryony, is it? and all your other New York chums. It'll be delightful. And I'm so pleased to hear you're still socializing," she added with unmistakeable chagrin in her voice. "I thought you'd be bored and lonely all by yourself, in a foreign country. Obviously not."

I decided not to give Alison the lonesomeness spiel and instead let her think that New York society more or less revolves around me. I rattled on shamelessly about Fay and Julia the camerawoman from L.A. to give the impression that I'm living an episode of **Sex and the City,** although this was probably a mistake, since my sister will be able to see on Friday for herself what a sad set of saps our friends really are. I painted Fay—a short workaholic with flat feet and round shoulders—as the sort of luscious lipsticked lesbian straight women swoon over, and (getting increasingly carried away) morphed Brianna (poor, feckless Brianna) into a Homeric Siren. It'll be just my luck if Alison was actually listening to me this time.

I can't quite believe she's coming. Why is she coming? Is it so she can tell herself (and everyone else) what a sweet generous soul she is, the sort of sister who'll drop everything and travel halfway round the world to minister to an afflicted sibling? Or is it so she can remind me that she's a much better mother? **I virtually burped my children out, Q, I can't imagine why you're having so**

much trouble. Perhaps you're not built for child rearing—hahahahahahaha....

32

My first memory of Alison is from the day my mother brought her home from the hospital. I was only two and a half, but I still recall staring in disbelief at her squished face, dark eyes, and ugly purple puffy hands. My mother looked at me over Alison's impossibly tiny body and told me I wasn't the baby anymore. From now on, she said, my job was to help look after the **new** baby ("I can't expect much from your father, dear"). I concluded, rightly, that my childhood was over. It hadn't lasted long.

My therapist asked me to bring in a photograph of Alison for one of our sessions. I chose a snapshot of us on a family holiday to Brittany in about 1979. We're standing on the beach, our arms around each other's waists, dressed in matching purple bathing suits with gold rings at the collarbone. Jeanie is slumped on the ground at our feet, distractedly playing with a pair of pink flip-flops. My mother is just out of the frame, although you can see her long shadow stretching across the sand in the late-afternoon sunshine.

My father was taking the photograph. There's a fuzziness in the top right corner because his index finger is over the lens.

The therapist asked me why I chose this particular photograph. I told him it was because Alison looked good in the suit and I looked terrible, and that I was angry at my mother for making us buy the same one (she couldn't be bothered to wait for me to try on a second suit, although she pretended she was giving me a character-building lesson. "Really, I'm surprised you're so concerned about how you look. Women have been defined by their looks for generations, dear. Nowadays we must strive to be defined by our brains, our achievements in the workplace." Fine, I said, I'll strive for that in about fifteen years, but now can I have that red suit with the ra-ra skirt and the white polka dots?).

In fact, that was only part of the truth. I didn't feel like pointing out to the therapist—it was his job to notice, surely—that Alison was pinching the flesh at my waist very hard with her right thumb and forefinger. "Come on you two," my father had said to us, "get a bit closer, can't you? Let's have a nice photo of the sisters." Alison and I glanced at each other with covert expressions of dislike, but we shuffled closer to each other obediently (we generally did what my father asked, I don't know why; perhaps we felt sorry for him). I felt Alison's arm snaking around my waist, and I slipped mine around hers in response—only then did I feel her deliberately take a fold of my skin just above my hip bone and squeeze. It really hurt. The second after the photograph was taken I thumped her, and my parents stopped my pocket money for two weeks as punishment. Which meant that I didn't have enough to buy the stripy Breton sweater I coveted, or the set of rainbow-colored pastels in a wooden box. So you see, the consequences of that pinch were far-reaching indeed.

I keep the photo on the bookcase, and so far the only person to detect Alison's malevolence was Tom. (There's a reason I married him.) He picked it up one day, stared at it with a frown deepening on his face, and then said, "She's got you good, hasn't she? Little bitch!" The therapist only glanced at the photograph and said something nonsensical about how cute I looked in the hated suit. I stopped visiting him after that.

33

I remember reading, in a class on feminist theory at university, a book about why women seem so much more involved with other women than men are with other men. Children are raised by their mothers in most Western societies, the author said, and mothers tend to experience themselves as like their daughters and unlike their sons. So boys grow up thinking of themselves as different, separate, autonomous, whereas girls think of themselves as like, connected, reliant. This early child-parent dynamic colors our relationships with friends, lovers, and family members throughout our lives.

My mother didn't think I was like her. Frankly, I wish she had. For most of my childhood she made it perfectly clear I was **not** like her. At your age, dear, she'd say, I was a trend setter, not a trend follower. The girls at school looked up to me, heck, they wanted to **be** me. What's wrong with you?

Alison, meanwhile, was elected school president in the biggest landslide in the history of our school, and within a few terms of arriving at Oxford she was a widely recognized "it" girl. My mother must be the only parent in history who took a sneaking delight in her daughter's cigarette addiction. She thought Alison looked tremendously cool in her black turtlenecks, the smoke of a glowing Camel curling up through her long eyelashes into her tousled dirty-blond hair. I heard them once having a conversation about magic mushrooms. As long as you quit before your midtwenties, or before you have children, I don't see the harm dear, my mother said, seriously. Youth is so fleeting. Grab the opportunities while they're there. Really, I wish I had.

Alison might have been number two daughter, but she made up the ground pretty fast. She's already got most of the boxes on the Modern Woman's List of Things to Do Before Hitting Thirty checked, and she's only just turned twenty-six.

34

Friday 7 P.M.

My party starts in an hour. The caterers are in the sitting room at this very moment. And my sister is in the spare room snoozing. She arrived an hour ago looking irritatingly cool and together. When I step off a plane I have a lank center parting, bloodshot eyes, and peeling dry skin. Alison is the kind of person who packs herself an elegant pouch with cosmetics to delight a magpie's eye: an azure water spritz bottle, an ice-pink pot of lip salve flavored with champagne rhubarb, an iridescent tube of mango-and-guava moisturizing cream.

Tom—who came home early from work to help oversee the party preparations, miracle of miracles—showed her into the sitting room. She kissed my cheek, kicked off her Italian leather flat-heeled shoes, and curled up cross-legged on the floor by my sofa. How was your flight? I asked, with the air of one who didn't give a damn.

Alison glanced at my sour expression out of the corner of her eye, paused, then turned on her most charming smile. "Q, lovely, be nice to me," she said, rubbing my hands with expensively manicured fingers. "I'm really happy to be here, and I'm **so** pleased to see you looking so well. Let's make a real effort to get on, okay?"

Which is typical of her. She always has to be the good guy.

"I don't know quite what you mean," I countered. "I only asked how your flight was."

Advantage Q.

Alison laughed her delicate laugh, the new one she's evolved since marrying the Honorable Gregory Farquhar and becoming a Faine Laidy. "Ah, Q—always the same, and that's why we love her," she said, with an incredibly irritating air of indulgent condescension. "Your sister's come halfway round the world to see you, and you're still in the glums, huh? Come on, sweetie, hopefully a few gifties will help pull you out of your funk. Here's a little something from Gregory and me, and this is from Mummy." She handed me two packages, one covered with stiff, boldly designed wrapping paper, the other with a wrinkled brown paper bag. Inside the first I found a Kate Spade makeup bag, inside the second a wheat-germ and lavender pillow. No prizes for guessing who sent what.

"Oh—Kate Spade," I said, airily. "Yes, this is one of her prettier designs, isn't it? She's a touch 1990s now, don't you think? But this little bag is charming, really charming," I added, brimming with insincere sincerity. I was determined to show her that I can afford my own designer accessories, thank you very much.

Alison blinked rapidly, two or three times. "Don't keep it if you don't want it," she said, mortification evident in the catch at the back of her throat (a hit! A palpable hit!). "I wanted to buy you something pretty, Q, and I know how frustrating it is when people either give you clothes that look like tents, or things you won't be able to wear for at least a year. I thought a little makeup bag was a good compromise." She paused and sniffed pathetically.

I looked at her pretty, flushed, down-turned face and felt like an absolute heel. I know when I'm being outplayed. "It was a very nice idea," I said reluctantly, conceding defeat. "Much better than this ridiculous wheat-germ pillow. What does Mummy think I am, a pregnant gerbil or something?" I said, playing (not very successfully, I'll admit) for laughs. Alison's face cleared immediately and she giggled dutifully, secure in her victory. "That's better, Q," she said, giving my knee a condescending pat. "That's **much** better, dear." I smiled tightly at her and moved my knee three millimeters to the left.

Now she's sleeping next door. And I'm wondering how I'm going to get through this evening, let alone the next week. I'm exhausted. Spending time with Alison drains me. As for parties—I hate throwing parties. Why did I do this? I hate feeling responsible for other people's pleasure.

35

Saturday 5 P.M.

The party was quite an event. My failures were numerous and varied. The first three that come to mind, in no particular order, are as follows:

1. Paola was completely uninterested in Fay. Instead, she took a real shine to Alison; they bonded fiercely over Art. At about ten o'clock, after Alison and Paola had been holed up for nearly two hours discussing the finalists for last year's Turner prize, I forced Tom to go and get Fay and introduce her into the conversation. Paola and Fay talked for all of seven minutes, at which point Fay realized that

she was de trop and excused herself. She sat in the corner looking pathetic and lonely for a quarter of an hour, then left without saying good-bye. Paola and Alison, meanwhile, parted with promises of eternal friendship.

2. Brianna and Alexis didn't actually meet, because Brianna left the party five minutes before he walked in. She walked out because she obviously couldn't handle being in the same room as Mark. As soon as he entered with Lara on his arm, she turned an extraordinary grayish green, hid in the bathroom for ten minutes, then bolted, leaving the unmistakeable stench of vomit behind her. I felt as if I'd just murdered a litter of orphaned kittens.

3. Alison said over breakfast, with a sparkle in her eye that jetlag could not extinguish, "My goodness, Q, I got the impression from talking to you that your friends were terribly—well—degenerate, if not absolutely debauched. But really, they're a very sober group, aren't they? Half of them didn't even drink! Dear me, when I think of how much alcohol Gregory's friends get through at our little dinner parties, and how naughty they become..."

She was right, I'm afraid. My party was desperately staid. I am no grand Victorian hostess, no Ottoline Morrell. I cannot claim to have united extravagant patrons and poets half-wild with hunger. Great Things were not said, opium was conspicuously absent, and I seriously doubt whether anyone left my halls last night and committed suicide. (I don't know if any of these things happened at Ottoline Morrell's parties, but I doubt she'd have been so famous if her guests had chomped their way stolidly through a few bags of pretzels and compared notes on their amicus briefs.)

And finally, more disastrous than any of the above, Tom and I had a huge row in the early hours of this morning. At midnight I heaved myself off the sofa and vanished into the bedroom, rubbing my eyes and pleading my belly; two hours later I was woken by "Bridge over Troubled Waters" frothily rendered through a mouthful of toothpaste. Too much Lagavulin, I thought to myself as I watched Tom solemnly drop his tooth-brush into the laundry basket and his underwear into the trash. The party was staid all right, but that didn't stop my overworked husband from polishing off three-quarters of a bottle of double-distilled scotch.

He stumbled heavily into the bedroom from the master bathroom a few moments later, blinking in the darkness. I propped myself up on my elbow and shook my head at him.

"You're drunk," I said, severely.

He peered at me. "Oh, there you are—**dah-ling,**" he said, in the faux English accent he tends to adopt when he's three times over the legal driving limit; and then, face twisted into a clown grin, "Aw-right, whassup guv?" he hiccupped tipsily.

My husband labors under the terrible misapprehension that his English accents are (a) good and (b) charming. They are, of course, face-smashingly irritating.

"For god's sake, get into bed and go to sleep, will you?" I snapped crossly, lying down again. "I need my rest." I yawned ostentatiously.

Abashed, Tom came and perched on the edge of the bed, looking earnestly down into my face. "You mad at me? Why mad at me? Please don't be..." He tailed off, rumpling his curly hair with a tragic expression. I took pity on him.

"All right," I said with a heavy sigh, rolling over to make more room for him under the covers. "I'm not mad, okay? Just get into bed, and tell me about the party. Who did you talk to?" He grinned happily, pulled back the comforter, and elbowed his way into bed, pulling my ass toward him and cupping my body in "spoons."

"Okay party, nice people, Mark happy, don't know 'bout Lara, think Patty's annoying..." he tailed off again, his breathing steadied, and for a moment I thought he was asleep, but then—

"That Alexis is an 'diot," he said, suddenly.

I opened my eyes in the darkness. "What?" I asked, surprised.

"Alexis, that his name? Pretty boy, blondey hair, floppy bangs? 'Diot," he repeated himself solemnly. "Total 'diot."

"But—why?" I asked.

He snuggled deeper into my neck. I could feel his breath, warm and smoky, on my skin. "You looked so good tonight, Q, sorta regal on your couch, and I love how shiny your hair is these days. Mmmmm, smells good too...What was I talkin' about—oh, yeah, Alexis. He told me about the building over the road, demolish—demol-ish—demolishment. Whassit. You know. Said they're going to stop it. Stupid. Not going to hap-pen. **Fucking** stupid, actually," he said with the air of one who was just beginning to fathom the reality of the situation. "Old people have to get their asses outta there. Big money on the line. Rent control a thing otha past. Told him so. Told him he doesn't know what he's doing." I stiffened, but Tom didn't seem to notice; instead he yawned hugely and slipped his hand comfortably over my right breast. "Anyway, I told him Randalls is a huge company, lotsa connections, good legal rep-resentation, no chance. Actually"—he chuck-led—"I didn't tell him this, but **we** represent their development interests, think Smyth and Westlon do their eviction stuff, Phil put me on their devel-opment por—por'folio jus' last week—"

His fingers were lazily circling my nipple. I firmly prized them off and sat bolt upright.

"You what?" I said. "**You what?**"

He looked up at me through heavy eyes. "We—what?" he repeated, stupidly. "Whaddya mean?"

"You represent Randalls?" I asked accusingly, staring down into his face, blurred by the drink and the darkness.

"Yeah," he replied, "'Course, we're, like, the best real estate firm in the city, whasso—I mean, so what?"

"So what? Christ, Tom, for your information, I happen to know that Randalls are total **bastards,** they're trying to force out a bunch of old people who've lived there for, like, forty years. Maybe rent control is a thing of the past, but these people are going to lose their homes, an entire community will be broken up—wait, you think that's **funny**?"

Because Tom was laughing. He was laughing as if what I was saying was just crassly, unbelievably silly. "Honey, wait up, Randalls is a business, they want to build, that's what they do, so—what're you so upset about? Nothing to you, you hardly know those people anyway—"

I stared down at him, feeling outraged, angry, confused. I opened my mouth to start trying to explain about Mrs. G and her friends, about the community that will be destroyed if they're scattered to the four corners of the city, but then I shut it again. Why **do** I care? Is it because Randalls aren't crossing their **i**'s and dotting their **t**'s? Is it because Mrs. G has been helping me and I want to do something for her in return? Or is it because I turn out to feel a terrible sympathy for people who don't understand the system, who aren't trained and educated to get the things they want?

Tom was still staring up at me, as if he'd found himself inexplicably in bed with the wrong woman. "Q, this is ridiculous, no one thinks rent control is a good thing anymore, you're British, maybe you don't get it"—he reached up to chuck my chin—"come lie down again, this is silly, come give me some lovin'—"

Tom represents Randalls. **Tom represents Randalls**. The thought of making love with him suddenly disgusted me. "You have to be kidding," I said, furiously, pushing his hand away. "My God, I feel like I don't **know** you anymore," upping the ante considerably, but I didn't care. "These days, Jesus, Tom, all you think about is your career, your firm, making money—is that all there is to you now?" I went on (feeling that I was on firmer ground at last). "All you care about is **you,** whether you're going to make partner, it makes me sick, it makes me just **sick**. You don't think about me, or the neighborhood, or the baby, or anyone but yourself. Fuck you, do you hear me? **Fuck you**. You can sleep on the fucking floor tonight as far as I'm concerned." And with that I rolled over, turning my shoulder sharply against him.

There was a long, long pause. I heard Tom breathing hard behind me. With an enormous effort I forced my own breath out slowly and quietly, pretending (quite implausibly) to be on the very edge of sleep. Finally I heard a low, furious, hissed **"I see,"** followed by the jolt of the bed as he got out, then the sounds of blankets and the yoga mat being pulled from the top shelf of the wardrobe and thrown onto the floor. A few moments later one of the pillows propped beneath my back was unceremoniously pulled from the bed (I squawked in spite of myself) and dropped heavily onto the mat. Tom settled himself into his small hard bed. We both lay and stared at the gray ceiling.

This morning, when I woke up, Tom was gone; the yoga mat and blankets were nowhere to be seen. I heard the sounds of movement in the kitchen, the clatter of plates, the thud of the fridge door slamming shut, and I called out to him to come to me—but, a moment later, Alison's unwanted head appeared around the door instead. "Oh you're awake," she said, bustling officiously into the room with a tray and settling it on my bedside table. I pulled the cover up to my chin and wished she was back on the other side of the hemisphere. "Here's coffee and croissants for the two of us, decaf for you of course, Tom declared he had a work emergency and vanished out the door at half-past seven. Flung himself out the door, more like, with a face black as thunder and eyes like two glowing coals. Having a barney, are we?" she added, with faux solicitude as she settled herself comfortably on the end of my bed, watching my face intently.

Needless to say, I denied anything was wrong and launched into a highly unconvincing monologue about how pregnancy had brought us closer together.

36

Tom and I met on a warm late-September Sunday afternoon four years ago, in a coffee shop just off Washington Square. I'd arrived in Manhattan two months earlier and was working my way down a list of friends and passing acquaintances who lived in the city, trying to make a new life for myself. Whitney was the cousin of a friend from university, and she was genuinely nice, a cheerful advertising executive with braided hair and a tiny diamond in her left nostril. (I never saw her again, because that night I slept with Tom and forgot everything and everybody I'd ever met. I found her telephone number in my wallet six months later, folded up between an ATM receipt and an old

Metro card, but by then the moment for friendship had passed.)

Whitney and I had just sat down and were en-
joying our lattes in the afternoon's amber sunshine when a man in his late twenties with a blunt
Caesar cut accosted us. Could he and his friend
join us? he asked, flashing us a glimpse of too-
white teeth and too-taut biceps as he smilingly
pulled out a chair, secure of our assent. Whitney
said something—I don't recall what now—but
as a putdown it was masterly. The man with the
Caesar cut shrugged casually, pushed in the steel
chair, and said something about "tight-assed
chicks" as he poured himself into a seat at the
next table. His friend—a quiet-looking, slender
man with curly black hair, sea-colored eyes, and a
beautifully tailored sports coat—looked horrified,
and when Caesar got up to buy a packet of ciga-
rettes, he came over and hurriedly apologized.

Whitney nodded vaguely at him as he spoke;
I don't think she even quite knew who he was,
but I'd been watching him covertly over the rim
of my glass since Caesar's intrusion. He wasn't
quite my type—not the type of the last few years,
anyway; I had a history of going for boyish-look-
ing blond men, usually about an inch shorter than
me and six months' younger. This man was dark,
tall, and quite obviously a grown-up; his clothes
were carefully chosen and carefully pressed, and
they looked expensive. He couldn't be more than

thirty, but he already had money. Businessman or lawyer, I pondered, before settling, after some thought, on lawyer. He had the faintly effete, intellectual look of a man who had considered academia but judiciously selected a career with better job opportunities, I decided—and I was right.

I discovered this a few hours later, sitting on a bench in Washington Square. Whitney and I had parted at the mouth of the subway at West Fourth with promises of friendship that were undermined from the outset by my deceitful claim to need the 6 uptown from Bleecker Street. When she was safely out of sight, I doubled back to the coffee shop, hoping to find him still there—and the gods favored me, because I arrived just as he was paying the check with a flourishing signature and a Mont Blanc pen. He looked up at me as I hovered uncertainly ten feet away from where he was sitting, then smiled, stood up, and walked over as if we'd arranged to meet all along. "My name's Tom," he said, extending his hand with an appealing combination of confidence and deference. "You're beautiful. Would you please take a walk with me?"

I remember Caesar gaping in surprise; I remember the touch of Tom's hand on the small of my back as he steered me across the road toward Washington Square. I remember passing the silent chess players encircling the park's entrance, the cacophony of barking as three dozen dogs tore round and round the dog run. I remember over-excited kids splashing about in the fountain, the faint hush of cool air playing in the gold-tinged leaves at the tops of the trees. I remember steal-ing secret glances at my companion's tanned skin and long eyelashes, his slender, capable hands.

We sat down on a bench near one of the en-closed play areas and watched children on swings sailing high up into the air, their nervous mothers in tight Gucci jeans clustered against the fence. Tom opened with another apology. Caesar was a former classmate from Harvard, he explained, a once-good friend who now worked for McKinsey, the management consultants. He didn't normally hang out with such superficial people, he assured me. The last time they had seen each other Daryl was still a shy nerdy math major, but money and position had changed everything. Tom told me he wouldn't be seeing Daryl again, and I think I fell in love with him at that moment because of the sweet severity in his eyes.

By that evening, I knew all about his family relationships (friendly), his college experience (good), his ambitions (serious), his last girlfriend (married), and everything I heard confirmed my initial impression. He was mature, hardwork-ing, established, available—everything a grown-up woman wants in a man. And everything she wants **from** a man too. The first three nights passed in a haze of sweaty, vaguely S&Mish sex that left me embarrassed but desperate for more. His teeth marks were at my throat, mine encircled his thighs. Then, on the fourth night of our relationship, he chose to be tender. I woke up the next morning knowing for certain I was going to be his wife.

I remember gazing at him over dark coffee and blueberry pancakes at the end of the first week and thinking to myself, on top of all this, he's **American**. I wasn't clear at the time why this was so important, but I knew that it was. Months later, half-drunk, I told a friend that one of my boyfriend's great charms was that he lived a long (long, long, long) way away from my mother.

We were married two years later in circumstances maximally designed to irritate her. The judge Tom clerked for performed the ceremony in his chambers, attended by just two witnesses (Mark, and a friend of mine from primary school, who happened to be visiting). Afterward the five of us sat down to brunch at our favorite place in the West Village and enjoyed cinnamon-sprinkled French toast before a crackling fire. Of course, this wasn't nearly romantic enough for my mother. As far as she was concerned, either we had to elope, preferably pursued by a wronged first wife, or host a grand affair at which she could swank about looking important. The second, of course, Alison had already provided, with her very fancy St. Margaret's Westminster wedding, and I strongly suspect Jeanie will manage the first (although I seriously doubt my mother will enjoy the reality of the thing. When she thinks of elopement she thinks of moonlit churches and a scape-grace aristo escaping his family's wrath, not Camden registry office with a pock-marked goon named Dave).

My mother found Tom bewildering from the very beginning. Until she met him, she preferred to pretend he didn't exist. Then, when we went to visit her in London and his physical presence rendered that strategy useless, she attempted to pretend he was actually English. And when Tom refused to play ball, calmly discussing congressional politics and possible judicial nominations for the Supreme Court, she decided war was inevitable and began an all-out campaign to convince me to drop him. "I don't know Q, I never thought you'd be one to **settle,**" she said, wide-eyed with pseudoconcern. "I thought you were the kind of girl who'd wait until the Right One came along. Biological clock ticking, is it dear?"

Her campaign failed, of course, and we got married, although one thing she said has been haunting me these last few weeks. "He's very handsome, but will he give you the space to **grow?**" she asked, when I called her to explain we'd been married that morning. "I'm fifty-six and I'm only just beginning to discover who I really am, Q. I had no time for self-discovery while

I was married, your father was too busy pursuing his own dreams to think of helping me with mine. I know you think I put my work first when you were growing up, but **somebody** had to earn the money to support us all. Well dear, your bed is made now, but all I can say is, I hope your new husband will listen to your dreams."

37

Monday 2 P.M.

"What **are** your dreams, Q?" This from Alison, over dinner last evening, which was unfortunately **à deux** because Tom worked right through the night.

Alison and I were eating leftover party food (which is guaranteed to put anyone into a bad mood), and she was telling me about some prize she'd recently won for an abstract sculpture of a cat. (It doesn't look anything like a cat, obviously. To wind her up I told her it looked more like a rabbit, but then to wind **me** up she said I'd detected that the piece complicates the whole nature of the relationship between predators and prey.)

"I mean, you got on the high school/university/law school track, and you never seemed to think about getting off. Do you really **want** to be a lawyer? You've come all the way over here to the States. Sometimes I wonder if you're actually hiding from us, so we won't see that you don't know what to do with your life. Am I wrong?" She lifted her eyes to mine; I saw the challenge sparking within them.

I met her gaze, levelly. "What on earth makes you think I don't want to be a lawyer?" I said, coolly.

"Well, you don't seem to care that bed rest keeps you from the office. I mean, I understand wanting a holiday, I understand wanting a break from the grind, but if I couldn't do my sculpture—don't snort, Q, it doesn't become you—I'd get really frustrated. Mummy would go mad if she couldn't teach her classes, Jeanie absolutely adores her master's courses, and I think Tom would tear out that curly hair of his if he couldn't be a lawyer. His job seems to absolutely consume him. But you—I don't think you give a damn, darling. You don't even seem to think about your work these days, not the way you used to think about your essays and things at Oxford, at least. That tells me you're not happy with your choice of career."

As you can imagine, my blood was boiling by this point. I was really mad, let me tell you. Listen, sister dear, I told her. We don't all have husbands who support us. Some of us work for a living. Yes indeedy. And just because I don't have some artsy-fartsy job doesn't mean I'm not fulfilled by what I do. I actually **help** people, which is more than can be said for your cats that look like rabbits and your pots that complicate the nature of the relationship between working and being bloody useless. Ha! What do you think of **that**? I flung at her, lip curled.

She shrugged and started to say something about how her art pushes at the boundaries of the normal, but I changed the subject. I didn't want to hear any more of her rubbish.

38

3 P.M.

It's not **true** that I don't think about work. Brianna keeps me upto-date on my old cases, Fay tells me about the new ones, and I've been helping Residents Against Demolition in their fight against the landlord. So there.

It is true that my work at Schuster doesn't occupy every sliver of my tortured soul the way Tom's work occupies his, but that's because I'm more balanced. Yes, that's it—I have a very balanced attitude to life. That's what I'll tell Alison the next time she brings it up.

4 P.M.

Alison denies I have a more balanced attitude to life. "Don't give me that nonsense, Q. You spend ninety hours a week at work. That's not balanced, now, is it? But you could convince me it was at least **reasonable** if you seemed to find it exciting, if it was obviously stimulating you. But I don't see anything of the sort. So what's going on, dear?"

I told her her stupid pots made me sick.

Tuesday 1:30 A.M., written in the light of my laptop screen

Tom and I have technically just made up. I say "technically" because, when I saw his shadow in the doorway an hour ago, I sat up in bed and said, in a voice that sounded perfunctory even to my ears, I'm sorry I flew off the handle on Saturday night. And he said, stilted, cool, ambiguous, **Yes, I'm sorry too**.

There was a pause. I wondered what to say, how to make things right again without giving in, without taking back the truth, the heart, the nut of the argument. And then he suddenly said, Look, Q, I'm exhausted, I don't have time for a big emotional thing with you right now, okay? I've hardly slept in two days. I'm just going to make up the mat on the floor again tonight, that way I won't disturb you and you won't disturb me.

Okay, I said, equally cool, **do what you want,** settling myself back into the bed with a theatrical flounce. With tightened lungs and tingling fingers, I lay and listened to him making up his thin narrow mat.

So now he's lying on his side on the floor five feet away from me, face turned away from the bed, a mop of dark hair just visible above the top of the blanket. I've been watching him sleep for the last half hour, wrapped up in a body that suddenly doesn't seem to belong to me anymore.

39

Wednesday 1 P.M.

It's incredibly windy today, and the sky is heavy and overcast. One of the old ladies in the apartment building opposite is trying to hang out her laundry, she's struggling to tie shirts on a makeshift line strung across her shallow balcony. Today's entertainment for a weary, heartsore Q.

Alison asked to see my baby purchases last night, and Tom-to my surprise—emerged from behind a stack of books and said he wanted to see them as well. So he and Alison fetched the boxes out of the nursery (aka the spare room, aka Alison's perfumed lair); Tom found a couple of pairs of scissors, and the two of them sliced and ripped and tore until the sitting room was overflowing with furniture, linens, ointments, toys, and a million pale blue Styrofoam chips. Alison praised my purchases effusively, and even Tom seemed affected by the sight of the tiny sea grass bassinet. Out of the corner of my eye I saw him lift one of the soft blue sheets gently to his cheek. It hardly seems possible that our baby son will be lying within them in a few weeks.

After dinner, Alison brought up the job topic again. It was horrible timing; looking at baby purchases had introduced a new flush of warmth into the atmosphere between Tom and me, a small return to intimacy. It wasn't much, but I felt a lightening in my chest all the same as Tom grinned at me over a teddy bear that plays "Moonlight" when you pull its ears. He took a real shine to it and sat fiddling with its curly golden coat all the way through the meal.

The subject of careers cooled things down immediately.

"Tom, do you think Q enjoys her job?" Alison asked, watching Tom closely as she sipped from a goblet of raspberry-hued Chilean red.

Tom, perched on the window bench, went very still. "What do you mean?" he asked, cautiously. I saw his knuckles whiten around his coffee cup.

Alison made a small moue with her red lip-sticked mouth. "She didn't tell you about our conversation?" she asked, her eyes darting between us; I knew what she was thinking. I felt anger welling up inside me.

"Alison lectured me the other day about my choice of employment, and she's under the delusion that her harangue was worth sharing with you, darling," I said to Tom, looking daggers at my sister. "It wasn't, obviously. I tell you everything important," I added, loudly, for her benefit.

Alison shrugged and looked Tom searchingly in the face. "I told Q that I don't think she's fulfilled by what she does. She used to love her work at school and at Oxford, now she barely seems to think about it. She disagreed with me, but I wonder what you think. You know her better than anyone these days," she said, with a faint but discernable emphasis on the last two words, as if to say, **she's a mystery to the rest of us**.

Tom stared at her, then at me. "Honestly, I don't know if she's 'fulfilled' or not," he said at last, slowly. "I think she might be happy in a different, less high-stress job, certainly."

Alison nodded energetically. She clearly thought she was on to something. "That's very interesting, Tom; I'm **very** interested that you said that," she said, looking over at me meaning-fully. She ran her fingertip around the rim of her glass speculatively, producing a low ringing hum. "And what about you?"

Tom was taken aback. "I'm sorry?" he said, politely. His voice seemed to be coming from somewhere on the other side of the city.

"Well, as I said to Q, it's obvious you really love your job, but you work **ungodly** hours. Frankly, I don't know how Q will manage when the baby comes, I think it'll be a real strain on her. So would **you** be happy in a less high-stress job, as you put it?"

I gasped, horrified; now he'd think **I'd** put her up to this, that I was complaining about him to my interfering, superior little sister, that I had asked her to intervene for me...

There was a silence. The wind was getting up; outside I heard the clatter of a newspaper vending machine crashing along the sidewalk, a faint indignant cry as someone lost a hat, the rush of last year's leaves swirling up the street, around the corner, into dust. Tom rose to his feet, putting down his espresso cup very gently on its tiny thin saucer. He smoothed down his trousers, glanced over at me with a look of—what was it? Reproach? Anger? Sadness?—then ostentatiously examined his watch. When he finally looked up, his face was expressionless.

"Ungodly hours or not, I have to finish writing something up in the office tonight, so I'm afraid you'll have to continue this little conversation without me," he said, with a hint of bite, a nip that drew the blood to the surface of my face. "Help Q to bed, and make sure she has plenty of water, would you? I'll see you in the morning," he added as he dropped a light cold kiss on my forehead. Ten seconds later the apartment door banged shut, and he was gone, out into the equinoctial gale.

Alison looked over at me, expectantly. I said nothing. There was nothing I could say without revealing to her the full extent of our problem, which seemed suddenly—**huge,** an anvil-shaped wedge formed from the aggregated tensions of the last few months. (Or was it **years**? Have they always been there, since the first day, the first night, collecting and dividing and growing like cancerous cells?) For an awful moment I thought she was going to ask me what was going on between us, but she seemed to think better of it, because she carefully put down her wineglass and came over to hoist me up off the sofa. "I'll fill your water jug," was all she said as she helped me shuffle across the floor to the bedroom.

40

Thursday Noon

Tom left for Tucson in the early hours of the morning; he's going to stop off in Baltimore on the way back to see his parents. "Alison'll be here to look after you," he said to me quickly, too quickly, when he first heard of her impending visit, "so there's no reason I can't go now, is there?" I shook my head slowly. "I suppose not," I said evenly, thinking, if you can't imagine a reason I'm damn well not going to give you one. (Somewhere in my mind's ear I heard the dull "ting" of the wedge, dulled steel against dulled steel, two unyielding objects striking each other.)

Not that Alison is doing much to look after me; in fact, she's out shopping. She read about a one-day sale at Bendel's in the **New York Times** this morning, and I've never seen the woman move so fast. She bumped into Mrs. G in the hallway on her way out. "Q, here's your friend to sit with you," she announced grandly, as if she had personally called Mrs. G and arranged for her to keep me company. "I'll be home in plenty of time for the trip to the doctor's this afternoon," she called, "and to make you lunch," she added extraloudly, clearly hoping that Mrs. G would see what an exemplary sister I have.

Not, it should be said, that Mrs. G was in much of a state to notice anything. She was in a terrible condition when she arrived. I've never seen her so distraught, never heard her accent so thickened with distress. I could barely understand a word of what she was saying. I had to get her to drink two glasses of Tom's scotch before she was calm enough to communicate with me.

The letter I drafted must have freaked out Randalls, because they've resorted to the most bizarre, not to say unethical, behavior to deal with their tenants. It seems that, within twenty-four hours of receiving the letter, they'd hired someone to look into the tenants' personal and financial histories; this person (according to Mrs. G, he's short, fat, and looks like a porpoise) has been interviewing relatives, checking police files, and quite literally poking his nose into the garbage in an effort to find out how to "persuade" the tenants to leave. Those with so much as a parking ticket unpaid have been threatened with dire sanctions; residents talk of dark meetings in underground parking garages, of a terrifying voice husking warnings of deportation and fines. It seems porpoise man told the tenants that if they breathed a word of his meetings to Mrs. G, he'd get the FBI on them. And the CIA. And the Department of Homeland Security. Poor Mrs. G couldn't figure out why her friends started tumbling from the action group like lemmings from a cliff, claiming they'd accept the terms of the original agreement from Randalls after all, and would she mind dropping the matter, please?

Hooray for Mrs. G, who said that as a matter of fact she did mind, and what in the world was going on? Porpoise man may be scary, but I think Mrs. G is scarier, and yesterday evening she frightened one poor old couple into ponying up the story. The couple's daughter-in-law worked illegally for three months as a waitress five years ago, and porpoise face persuaded them that he'd have her green card application denied, thereby separating her eternally from her little boy, who was born at Mount Sinai last year and is a bona fide American citizen. The couple folded like a tent in a hurricane. According to Mrs. G, yesterday they were on the verge of signing a lease to an apartment that's a quarter the size of their current place and fifty blocks to the north.

This cannot be right, she told me, heatedly; it **cannot** be right. And I had to agree. It cannot be right.

As I listened to her talk, I stared before me, out the window, thinking deeply. Crimpson represents Randalls—not their eviction proceedings, true, but their development interests. If I support Mrs. G in this, if I work with her to expose Randalls, I'm going to be working actively against Tom—against his company, against his client, against (if you think about it) his whole view of the world.

"Mrs. G," I said to her abruptly, before I could change my mind, "I'm going to help you out, okay? You're not in this alone, I promise. I'm going to do some research, I'll figure out the details of your legal position. We're going to beat these bastards. I can't promise you your friends will keep their homes, but I'll make damn sure Randalls get their comeuppance and your friends get everything—all the money, all the legal protection—they're entitled to."

Mrs. G nodded slowly, relief smoothing away the harshest, darkest lines around her mouth. "You sweet girl," she said. "You very nice girl." I reached out my hand and lightly touched her shoulder, filled with the pleasing sense of working in tandem with someone, the two of us pulling together. She needs me, and I can help her.

But as the door closed behind her a cold feeling of panic swept through me. I've just pledged myself to help a group opposed to my husband's client—when my husband and I are hardly talking, when I'm heavily pregnant with our child, when I'm confined to bed to safeguard the baby's health. What have I **done**? What on **earth** have I done?

41

3 P.M.

At least the baby responded well to the nonstress test and ultrasound today. Dr. Weinberg was noticeably cheerful at the end of my appointment. "I'm giving him a ten-out-of-ten this time," she told me, heartily. "Before you know it he'll be graduating summa cum laude from Yale, or is it Harvard your husband attended? Harvard—that's right, I remember now, Harvard. **Oy oy oy,** he's a chip off the old block, this little one, if I'm any judge," she added, a warm twinkle in her eye.

I smiled tightly at her and said nothing. After the appointment I waited downstairs in the lobby of Dr. Weinberg's building while Alison hailed a cab, then I slowly heaved myself into the early spring sunshine. As I stumbled toward the taxi, blinking in the clear hard light, I caught sight of myself in the windshield. Six weeks without exercise does little for your body. My neck and throat have filled out, my face is rounded, my chest and belly seem to have merged into one vast protuberance. I felt the tears prickling at my eyelashes, the blood heating my cheeks. I barely recognize myself.

I used to be the kind of person people call "slim." **Slim** is one of those words you use to describe other people; it sounds very odd if you apply it to yourself, unless you're composing an ad for match.com. **Attractive** is another such word. I am also, as it happens, the sort of person people call "attractive."

My friends at university often wondered why someone like me—tall, slim, attractive—was usually single. It never seemed that odd to me. I'm perfectly pretty, but I lack that certain something—what is it? Sex appeal? Maybe. As the old expression goes, I don't know what it is, but I know it when I see it. My friend Lynn at school had it; true, she had braces wired across her teeth and acne troubling her chin, but you only had to watch her dance. She had total confidence in her body, as if she was utterly in charge of it, as if it held no secrets for her. Whereas I've always regarded mine with some bewilderment, its mysterious activities, its dark places where the blood flows close to the surface.

Still, while I was never the kind of girl men swoon over, Tom was not the first to fall for me. I am, after all, tall and slim; realizing the value of the latter, especially when combined with the former, I worked hard to keep my passionate love of all things sweet firmly under control. And so most people called me "attractive." Not beautiful—only Tom has ever thought that—but definitely, comfortably, attractive.

But now...well. I'm no longer slim, and I'm not just talking about my huge belly. I'm not even talking about the jowls of the last few weeks. As soon as I got pregnant my need for food became insatiable. All my life I've been able to keep my appetite at bay, but as soon as my body registered the new life, it began to demand cookies, cakes, fries, and all things blubber-inducing with an extraordinary intensity. And so the pounds piled on; at my monthly visits to Dr. Weinberg's I'd avert my gaze from the weighing machine, stop my ears as the nurse muttered "155," "162," "170." Then, of course, came bed rest, which put an end to my walks at lunch, my weekend perambulations in the park, not to mention my once-in-a-blue-moon trips to the gym with Patty. I'm now fifty pounds heavier than when I began, and I'm no longer "attractive." I don't need a glance in a taxicab window to tell me that. Slack-skinned around the arms and chin, my flesh is a grubby winter-white, and my frizzy hair is pressed flat on the left side of my head from all these endless days in bed. I'm huge, and an embarrassingly small proportion of my girth is child. At this rate I'll hit thirty with an SUV-size spare tire.

Is it any wonder my husband spends his nights at work these days?

6:30 P.M.

I've just had an extraordinary visit from Mark. I was lying on the sofa, typing this, fingers peeping out of our scratchy blue-and-gray wool blanket, when someone knocked on the door.

Alison had changed her mind about a frock from Bendel's and rushed back to exchange it ("I think I need the four, darling, just **look** at these folds of extra fabric"), so I was all alone.

"Q, I, er, hope this is an okay time," Mark said uncomfortably as he shook off his black leather jacket, peeled off a yellow cashmere scarf, and lowered himself into the leather armchair.

"It's a fine time," I said, dragging my thoughts to the present moment. Mark comes here to visit Tom, never me. "What can I do for you?"

"Come out and say—what?" I prompted, thinking, get it over with and get out of here. I quite dislike you.

I waited, expectantly. The moments passed; he said nothing. He stared at me like a discombobulated rabbit, his mouth slightly agape. I noticed that one of his two front teeth is slightly discolored.

"The thing is. The thing is—this," he said hesitantly, then all in a rush, "Q, I've been having an affair."

I sighed and resisted the urge to say, yes I know. It seemed like a time to play my cards close to my chest. "Really?" I said, summoning up tones of surprise.

"Yes, really, and the thing is, she—my…girl-friend was at your party. Last Friday. I saw her when I first walked in, but then she—she vanished. She's got long dark hair and cute freckles, and she was wearing a red dress with these thin little straps, and her name is—her name is—"

"Bri-**anna**?" I finished for him, with the air of one making a momentous discovery.

"Exactly." He gave two or three quick little nods.

There was a pause.

"I'm not sure why you're telling me this," I said at last, into the silence.

"Because I want you to help me get her **back**," he said, the words tumbling out at speed, and as he spoke he got to his feet and began pacing the floor, rucking up the edge of the Persian kilim as he did so. "I've been calling her every day, three times a day, since last Friday, and she won't return my calls. I'm going crazy. I love her, Q. I want her back. I'm going to tell Lara I want a divorce. I think I want to marry Brianna. Will you help me?" he finished, turning with a look of hopeful appeal on his face.

I have to admit, I called this relationship all wrong. As I gazed at him I suddenly realized that I was angry. Not just a little bit angry, but very, very angry indeed.

"Isn't there something you're forgetting?" I said, tightly. "A little matter of two kids and a pregnant wife?"

Mark ran his fingers helplessly through his thinning hair. "I know, I know, and I feel terrible about them. But, Q, I can't live a lie," he went on, unctuously. "I can't pretend to love Lara anymore. These days she's so **put together,** Q, you've no idea. Brianna is warm, and cozy, and loving. There's nothing I can do—"

"Nothing you can do? Don't give me that!" I said furiously—and before I knew what was happening the words were pouring out of me like lava from a long pent-up volcano. I don't remember much of what I said, but his staggered expression is imprinted on my mind's eye. The conversation ended with him storming out the door, swearing he had no idea why he'd confided in me, that I was the least sympathetic woman he'd ever met, and that Tom was a saint for putting up with me.

The door banged shut. I listened to the sound reverberate around the apartment. I do that a lot these days.

The phone intruded into the silence. **Beeep**. Pause. **Beeep**. Pause. That curiously American sound. It was my mother, her curiously English tones traveling across the Atlantic, through the long eely cable that connects us.

"Q, I have a surprise for you," she said, in pregnant tones.

"Yes?" I said, wearily. I was emotionally spent.

"Is that all you can say?" she asked, hurt. I took a deep breath, pulled myself together, and dutifully asked what the surprise was.

"I'm coming to stay with you until the birth!" she announced, and I actually dropped the phone; it literally fell out of my nerveless fingers. I stared at it, a lump of black plastic lying on the sofa's edge, and debated whether to pick it up or simply hit the "end" button and make her go away, possibly forever.

Of course I didn't hit the button. Instead, I briefly closed my aching eyes, then picked it up again. "Sorry about that, something wrong with the line," I said, unconvincingly. "Go on."

She sounded suspicious, offended, and eager all at once. "I hope you're pleased, Q. It's been a nightmare, finding teachers to cover at the studio, but people have rallied round and I've got the rota covered. I'm coming out on the nineteenth. You'll be, let me see, thirty-four weeks pregnant by then, and I can stay for two weeks at least, so I'll be there to see the baby!" she finished, in a voice bursting with excitement.

Coming out to visit me? In America? In New York? I couldn't believe what I was hearing. And suddenly I felt something I haven't felt in years, a yearning for her I cannot describe. **My mother**. Here. At last. But all I said was, great. Thanks. It'll be nice to see you.

Alison arrived home half an hour later with a teeny-weeny dress and fingernails freshly mani-cured and polished with matte peach paint. Over a cup of tea, I told her about our mother's plan to visit. She confirmed that Mum has been working to find teachers to cover her classes at the studio for the last three weeks. "She begged me not to say anything until she was sure she had everything organized. She wanted to surprise you," Alison said, then went on with a sniff: "she only visited me for two days after Serena was born. She swore she couldn't take time away from work, and I only live in London. But your pregnancy **has** been tricky, I suppose that's why."

I examined Alison over my Earl Grey and wondered if we'd ever grow up.

42

Friday 1 P.M.

I woke up this morning and glanced over at the empty place beside me in the bed. The large ex-panse of white sheet looked back at me, innocent-ly, defying the resentful thoughts gathering at the back of my just-conscious mind. It's hard to be angry with a bare white sheet.

Then my gaze traveled across the room, to the wooden chair by the door to the master bathroom. A pair of Calvin Klein underpants were slung across the padded seat, legs uppermost, a sloppy figure eight in gray wrinkled cotton. Come over here and pick us up and put us in the laundry basket, they said to me, irritably, and hurry up, we've been here two days already. You just lie around all day while we get up, go to work, and do all that important stuff. Come on, why don't you do a little something to earn your keep?

Sod you, I told them sullenly as I levered myself out of the bed. You can find your own way, I have my own things to do, as it happens. You're not the only ones with a job.

After breakfast I opened the computer and cracked my knuckles. Time for research.

Once upon a time, an investigation into rent control, rent administration, and the procedures required for demolishing buildings in New York City would have meant a day in a musty library scaling vertiginous shelves for huge tomes with gold-tooled bindings, tissue-paper pages, and microscopic print. Today, armed with a trusty Westlaw password, a woman on bed rest can figure out a surprising amount in about three hours.

The first discovery came quickly. I cut and pasted into a Word document: **The law prohibits harassment of rent regulated tenants.**

Owners found guilty of intentional actions to force a tenant to vacate an apartment may be subject to both civil and criminal penalties. Owners found guilty of tenant harassment for acts committed on or after July 19, 1997, are subject to fines of up to $5,000 for each violation. I saved the paragraph in a brand-new file called "Fuck Randalls" and then, as an afterthought, created a folder to house it titled (genteelly enough) "Randalls Discoveries."

Then I worked my way through the procedures "pursuant to the rent regulation code for the filing of an owner's application to refuse to renew leases on the grounds of demolition implementing emergency tenant protection regulations." (I've always rather liked lawyer's English, the Shakespearean use of words like **pursuant** makes me think of dark foggy alleyways, rapiers at night, a twist of parchment in a dead man's hand.) I highlighted, and cut, and pasted; I searched, I followed links, I created subsection upon subsection in "Fuck Randalls," and a pretty list of documents to nestle beside it in "Randalls Discoveries" (to wit, "Sod You Randalls," "No Way Randalls," "Randalls Are Dead Meat," etc. etc. etc.). To summarize: Randalls' buyout offers fall woefully beneath the stipends required by law, and the tenants have not been given the requisite paperwork. And while we're on the subject of paperwork—I pondered to myself, picking up the telephone at last—just where is that approval notice from the DHCR?

It took me a while and a few vaguely deceitful assertions (I am technically still an employee at Schuster, so it wasn't **much** of a lie) to discover what I'd long suspected—that Randalls's application to tear down the apartment complex has not yet been approved. In fact, it's due to be heard next month. Which means that there will be ample opportunity for the tenants' legal representatives to contest the application **and** to make the landlord's execrable behavior public. Time to find the tenants reliable legal representation.

I picked up the phone and called Fay. This is the situation, I told her. I want Schuster to take on a case pro bono. I'm going to e-mail you a letter, and I want you to sign it, and then send it to a company called Randalls. We'll also send a copy to both Smyth and Westlon and Crimpson Thwaite, their legal representatives. We're going to threaten everything from thunderbolts to the electric chair, and we're going to do it for a group of little old Greek ladies and gentlemen, for absolutely no money at all. Okay?

What Fay said is not worth repeating, but at the end of the conversation, my point was won.

I've never been terribly good at standing up for myself. And frankly, I've never been particularly good at standing up for my clients either; if

I'm truthful, I'm not an especially gifted firm lawyer. Which is odd, because I did well at university
and law school, better even than Tom, but he's
the one who ended up at Crimpson. Why is that?
It's struck me these last few weeks, as I've been
lying here, that I've never managed to **care** very
deeply about the people I'm supposedly helping.
I find it almost impossible to worry about a client
who's already doing well: if they can afford to hire
Schuster, well, they can't be suffering that much.
But these old people are different, they **are** suffering, and they have rights; the law is expressly
designed to protect them. I won't stand by and
see their rights ignored.

Well, that's the pitch I'm going to make to
Tom, anyway. Once the conversation with Fay
was done, thoughts of my absent husband slipped
unbidden back into my mind. Let's face it, one
day—soon—he's going to know about all of this.
He's going to think I'm meddling in things I
don't properly understand, he'll say I'm foolish
and sentimental. He may even think I'm working
with Mrs. G and Alexis deliberately to get back
at him, to derail his client, to embarrass him with
his partners.

I can't help that.

If, when he gets back from his trip, he asks
me what I've been up to, I will tell him. I'm not a
deceitful person by nature. Certainly not. I'll tell
him everything—**if** he asks. But I'm not going to

say anything unless he approaches me first, unless he says "Q, we've had some silly fights recently, but I love you, we're having a baby, I want us on the same page. So what's up with you?" If he says those words, then fine. If not—not.

43

Monday 7 A.M.

I'm thirty-three weeks' pregnant today. Tom has been gone for four days. Alison has been here for ten days. I've been awake for three hours. I last threw up twenty minutes ago.

Tom called late yesterday evening, from Baltimore; Alison was in the room at the time, so I conjured up my brightest smile, asked after my in-laws, and tried to conceal from my sister the fact that I was shaking with a cold nausea, a horrible shivering sensation deep in my gut.

Tom's almost hysterically cheery tones told me that his parents were within hearing distance as well. "The baby's good, yeah? Everything's going fine?" he asked, painfully upbeat. Alison's presence notwithstanding, I rolled my eyes. Why do people think a pregnant woman has some mysterious insight into how her fetus is doing? "Well, I asked him this morning, you know, and he said he was doing swimmingly, bit bored though," I told him sarcastically, and then (conscious of Alison's sharp little eyes), I laughed. "Haha. My joke. I mean, I felt him kick this morning, if that's what you mean. And how's that lease coming along?" I asked civilly, adding, as if compelled, "have you managed to screw any local residents down there? Destroy a few landmarks with a redbrick box? Hahaha! My joke!" I added, to cover up the venom. I smiled hugely at Alison as if to say, really, it's just nonstop lively repartee in our household.

Tom took a sharp breath. "Fuck you, Q," he said, low, furious, and then, as if someone had just walked into the room, "hahahaha! **My** joke. Funny, funny. That was **sooo** funny."

Things suddenly seemed to have gone too far. We discussed the arrangements for Tom's flight home in extensive detail and with extraordinary politeness for the next fifteen minutes while Alison flicked through her magazine pages (**thwack! thwack!**) and tapped her foot rapidly on the wooden floor. "Well, darling, I can't wait to see you," I finished, blandly.

"You too, my love," he replied, with equal blandness. "Really, I can't wait to be home." Click.

Mrs. G came to see me yesterday afternoon after church, accompanied by Alexis, who asked, with evident discomfort, if he'd caused trouble between me and Tom. He realized at the party that my husband didn't know about my involvement with the residents' action group (not, of course, that he realized the other thing, the fact that Tom himself represents Randalls, that I'm sleeping with the enemy, so to speak). I laughed lightly, cheerily. Of course it wasn't a problem, I said, conscious once again of Alison's needling eyes; Tom doesn't mind, no really, it's not a problem. Not a problem at all. Alexis was still looking anxious, but I firmly changed the subject to basketball—I've been watching it a lot these last few days, it annoys Alison no end—and he fell in with my lead. We talked about the kinds of skills Europeans bring to the NBA while Mrs. G snoozed and Alison drummed her sheared fingernails angrily against the table.

After about ten minutes, Alison got up to take a bath. Casting an eye at his still-sleeping aunt, Alexis leaned his dark-golden head forward and said to me, in a conspiratorial whisper, "That girl I met here the other day, your friend, Brianna...I hope you don't mind me asking, but is she single?"

I breathed in his smell of soap and skin, of dry-cleaned laundry and peppermint shampoo. (The smell of man. I miss that smell.) "You know, I think she is," I told him, leaning slightly closer. I could see the pink beneath his golden skin, the one long hair in his right eyebrow, the tiny scar on his forehead, an inch or so below his hairline. "Why, are you interested?"

He blushed and gave me an embarrassed half-grin. "I am, actually. I mean, I was thinking of asking her out to dinner, but I didn't see her at your party. I was sort of hoping—Well. If you can maybe give me her phone number, then I—y'know—" He trailed off as his face flushed deeper and deeper red.

I smiled at his awkwardness, then quickly scribbled Bri's number down; I told him I thought he should get in touch with her as soon as possible. Bri is obviously resisting Mark's attentions, so now is a good time to approach her, before her resolve weakens. Not that I explained this to Alexis, of course; I told him simply that I approved of his taste in women and, as his aunt snorted herself awake, that I was confident Brianna would agree to have dinner with him.

There's something very sexy about helping two people get their relationship started. It's got something to do with all that pent-up desire, I suppose, waiting to explode. It makes me remember those incredible first few days with Tom. (The first time I touched his skin, smooth as caramel. The first time I unbuttoned his cotton shirt and felt the hard warmth of his chest. The first time he kissed me until my bones shook. The first time I kissed him until his blue-green eyes lost focus and turned slate gray.)

I reread Austen's **Emma** over the weekend. I can't think why she had such trouble with matchmaking; it's a piece of cake. I think I'm going to go ahead and check the "unite lonely, single friends" box on my Modern Woman's List today. This one's definitely in the bag.

10 A.M.

Or—not.

I've just had a phone call from Brianna. She wants to get back together with Mark.

"You're not going to believe this," she began, "but it turns out **you know my ex-lover!**"

Really, I said, wearily slipping back into the role of kindly-but-oblivious friend. You do surprise me.

Yes, she told me; I saw him at your party. His name is Mark Kerry.

Heavens above. Good lord. I'm staggered.

"I knew you would be," she said. "Well, it's like this: he's been calling me for a week, ever since your party. Every day. Many times a day, actually. I haven't been returning his calls, not because I don't want to, but because I want to make sure he really wants me. I wouldn't go back to him if this is just an impulse thing, it's not fair to his wife, is it? But you know, I think he really loves me. In a message yesterday afternoon he told me he adores me, he said there's something he wants to tell me—what do you think it could be, Q? Do you think he's going to leave his wife after all? I mean, maybe I'm jumping the gun here, but the way he said it, I couldn't help wondering…"

I listened to her speculations with rising horror. (And, if I'm going to be frank, some concern about my own reputation for truthfulness. If they get back together, Brianna's going to realize that I've known about her relationship for a week now, she may even guess I've known about it for longer. Not that this is the most important thing on my mind right now, but still.)

Brianna, I cut in, I know his wife, okay? I **know** Lara. She's a friend—well, almost. I can't sit by and watch you take off with her husband. She's pregnant and she's got two kids, and—and look (with rising desperation), Alexis was here earlier today, he asked for your number, he's going to call you, and he's **so hot,** he has gorgeous eyes, lovely hair, and he's really nice, too—

"Q," Bri said, surprised, "sounds to me like **you** have a crush on this guy, but as for me, I'm afraid it's no good, I'm not interested, Mark is The One. I'll understand if you feel like you can't stay friends with me, but when Mark calls next, I'm going to pick up the phone and say yes to whatever he asks of me. **Whatever** he asks of me," she repeated, slowly, meaningfully. I hung up the phone.

But as soon as I did, I started to panic. Brianna is a good friend; she's also, let's face it, my most devoted visitor. Who will bring me yummy lunches and afternoon cookies, if not Brianna? Who will whisper details of sexy nighttime dalliances, if not Brianna? Who will ask my advice on the intricate steps in the romantic dance, if not Brianna? And who will listen sympathetically to **my** problems, if not Brianna?

Without Brianna I'm left with Alison. I picked up the phone and called her back.

Bri, I said, we're friends, right? I don't want to judge too hastily. Come and see me this evening and we'll talk things through. But then she told me she couldn't. Mark had left a message on her voice mail while she and I were talking, asking her to meet him for dinner at Le Bernardin.

What am I supposed to do now? Call Lara? Call Mark? Call Tom?

5 P.M.

Tom is due home from Baltimore tonight. Alison leaves tomorrow for England. So my husband and I will soon be together, alone, once again.

I feel like a taut string, like the E on a violin, bright silver stretched to the very edge of snapping. The peg turns and turns, the notes rise higher and higher.

My left index finger is bleeding heavily; I've spent the last half hour watching the blood soak through a succession of pink tissues. I cut it the other day trying to open an apple (it's hard to use a paring knife while lying on your side). I need a new Band-Aid, but there's no one to fetch it for me. Alison is shopping again. I seem to be falling apart.

44

Tuesday 6 P.M.

Alison's flight departs from JFK at 9 P.M. this evening. She left here a few moments ago with two new Louis Vuitton suitcases overflowing with luxurious purchases—a Dior evening dress in green silk, cashmere sweaters in every hue, an ebony bangle and a pair of earrings from Tiffany, an array of gorgeous silk ties for Gregory, stuffed toys for the kids, and that's just the contents of case number one. Her meddling advice, I hasten to add, has stayed here with me.

"I think you married Tom because you thought he was the kind of man Mummy would like," she said over breakfast this morning. Ha—that shows what you know, I said, as I worked my way through a battered, buttered croissant. Mummy absolutely loathed Tom in the beginning, I told her, embarking on a flaky oversize pain au chocolat.

"I know," Alison replied, meditatively, "but still, I think part of you wanted to find a professional man to get her approval, while the other part wanted someone she'd absolutely hate. What did you end up with? An American lawyer. You've always been split, Q, in your relationship with Mummy. You're half-desperate for her love, half-desperate to make her hate you so you don't have to feel guilty about hating her. You've been like that ever since we were little girls."

"How much is your counselor costing you?" I asked, solicitously. "I mean, I take it that's the source of all this psychological claptrap?"

"You're so aggressive," she said, evenly. "You're aggressive because you're deathly competitive with me. It was incredibly confusing when we were kids, Q. You were sweet to me when you wanted to make Jeanie feel bad and awful when Mummy made **you** feel bad. I'll admit it, as it happens, I **have** been seeing a counselor, and I was sad to hear you stopped seeing your therapist last year, Q. I think you have a lot of stuff to sort out, if you don't mind me saying so."

I did mind it, as I tried to tell her, but she was already well into the topic of "how are you going to bring up a child with a husband who's never home." "Thing is, Q," she went on seriously, "I was here for ten days and I saw him—what was it? For about three consecutive hours. He uses this place as a hotel. Is that really acceptable to you, darling? How are you going to cope on your own when the baby's been screaming for five hours straight?"

"Is there anything about my life you approve of?" I asked her sarcastically, wondering why on earth a woman with no discernable talent, a lumpen deadweight of a husband, and two unbearable children was lecturing **me**—again—on the state of my existence.

"I'll be interested to hear what Mummy has to say," she said severely, and my eyes rolled back in my head. Oh God, why did I ever think I wanted the woman here—is it too late to stop her from coming?

Alison was still talking. "I know you don't think much of Gregory, dear, you've made that perfectly clear, but we have an arrangement that suits us beautifully, and he supports my sculpting one hundred and ten percent. We have a peaceful home, I see my children all the time, and I enjoy my profession. Really, Q, I don't think you're on strong enough ground to be as judgmental as you are. And while we're on the subject, you've been horrid to Jeanie about Dave. He's not as bad as all that, and as far as I can tell you've spent very little time in his company."

The worst thing, of course, is that she has a point. Many points. I **am** horrible about Dave, it **isn't** my place to criticize Gregory, and my husband is, indeed, rarely at home. And, while we're at it, my friends are boring, my parties are tiresome, and my career doesn't interest me. Good God, Alison, I told her, you must come out and see me more often. I can really count on you to cheer me up.

As for Tom? He and I have been stepping around each other carefully, oh so carefully, ever since he walked through the door last night at 7:50. He deposited a box of Godiva chocolates into my lap with a half-glance at Alison. He thanked her for taking care of me in his absence with gentlemanly good manners. Then he slept the night on the far side of the bed, and to my knowledge, our skin never so much as touched.

45

I took PPE at university, but I had always wanted to study literature. Politics, philosophy, and economics were useful subjects, my mother said. They would show any potential employer that I was a Serious Person. With those subjects under your belt, she said, you'll be able to go anywhere, do anything. Doors will open to you. People will listen to you. But literature—literature! That's almost as bad as media studies, or home economics, or some other such "soft" discipline. (This was before she discovered personal enlightenment in the downward-facing dog, of course.)

So I took PPE, but I snuck into a few classes on poetry and fiction and literary theory. I always loved women's writing—the Brontës, George Eliot, Emily Dickinson, Kate Chopin, Virginia Woolf, Sylvia Plath—so many of them so tragic, their lives, their heroines' lives, ending in disaster, in the suck of the sea, gasping for air, the world closing over their heads in a moment of numbing release. Sometimes I would lie in my bedroom, face down into the carpet, and imagine that I was drowning in the river that flowed about half a mile from our house. I would close my eyes, let myself become heavy, and feel the darkness take charge. Half of me truly wanted to die, but without the pain, without the choking and the panic. This was my fantasy of death—death without untidiness.

There was a boy who lived two doors down from us who hanged himself a few months before our father left. The two events are connected in my memory. The landscape of my childhood changed that raw spring; by the time the peonies bloomed along the front fence, I knew I was finally grown up. The boy hanged himself because he was bullied, or at least that was the gossip among the kids at school. His name was Patrick, and he was a slight child, blond, and very pale. He hanged himself in the garden shed, a place where he rarely played, so it was twenty-four hours before his parents even found him. His face was purple, so the neighborhood kids said, and his tongue was black, and the metal wire he'd used to strangle himself almost took off his head. I used to wonder why he hadn't simply tied a few bricks around his waist and taken a final dip into the river. I suppose it was revenge on the parents who failed to protect him; personally I always thought the effect of an unsullied corpse would be greater. **See how perfect I am; see what you failed to appreciate**.

Then my father left, and I wondered for a few weeks if he'd committed suicide as well, and my mother was making the whole thing up. Or perhaps she'd killed him. But the simultaneous disappearance of our next-door neighbor's wife seemed to put paid to that idea, unless there'd been a complete massacre, and even I didn't think my mother had it in her to be a serial killer. Anyway, after a pause, he began to call us and send us letters, so it seemed likely that he was really still alive. I was a bit disappointed.

As a teenager I devoured books about absent and inadequate fathers, and there were plenty to choose from. Fathers who didn't protect their daughters, fathers who didn't understand their daughters, fathers who left their daughters. **Daddy, daddy, you bastard, I'm through**. Fathers who went off to war (**Little Women**), secreted themselves in the library (**Pride and Prejudice**), got violent (**Wuthering Heights**), provided conspicuously inappropriate stepmothers (don't get me started on fairy tales). Mothers are invariably annoying, but unless they expire in childbirth, they tend to stick around. Fathers are a whole 'nother story.

When fathers realize their life isn't going right, they take off.

46

Wednesday 7:30 P.M.

I was watching an elderly couple eating dinner together in the building opposite when Brianna arrived, her face flushed and softened with love fulfilled.

"We had the most amazing evening yesterday at Le Bernardin, Q, I can't even tell you," she told me, her eyes alight at the memory. "Mark's never been so tender. Halfway through the meal he told me he thinks he wants to spend the rest of his life with me. I know how you feel about Lara—Mark told me you'd had a fight with him about it, but I said I thought you were willing to make peace. You are, aren't you? **Please** say you are, Q. You've become such a good friend, I want you to be happy for me. I want you to be happy for Mark."

I stared at her. It seems that, in her hazy, love-drugged state, she hasn't quite tumbled to my duplicity. But that hardly matters now. I have to decide if I'm willing to throw over the only real friend I have these days, my only friend in a foreign country, in favor of—what? A woman I don't even like? Or the principle that you don't leave a pregnant woman to raise the kids on her own?

My son kicks and kicks, and we lie together contemplating our future. I can feel his head, the curve of his spine, the rounded shape of his buttocks through my stomach. I long to see him in his own skin. Although given the situation between his parents I suspect he's better off where he is, snuggled up under mine.

47

Thursday Noon

This morning I went to Dr. Weinberg's office for another ultrasound. The baby has kicked himself into a breech position.

I noticed a strange breathlessness when I tried to get out of bed this morning, and a new hardness under my ribs. The baby's head is now lodged snugly beneath them, a matter of inches from my heart. Dr. Weinberg tells me that, unless he moves again, he'll be born by cesarean section.

Tom decided, at the last minute, to come with me, and I thought—perhaps it was only fancy— there was a shade of relief in Dr. Weinberg's eyes when she saw him walk into the office, swinging his briefcase. When we learned of the baby's new position he reached out and grasped my hand. I jumped a little at the unexpected pressure, the warm skin touching mine. Surely the baby may shift again, he said to Dr. Weinberg in a low, urgent voice, and then he can be delivered normally? Dr. Weinberg shrugged. "Of course," she agreed, "although babies surrounded by so little amniotic fluid don't have much room to maneuver. It's a miracle he shifted at all," she added. "He's a determined one, this baby, I'm sure of it. He'll keep you guessing."

I wondered what Tom was thinking. It is testament to the state of our relationship that I truly do not know.

Cesarean section—major surgery. I will be cut open, the baby lifted out. Part of me is relieved— I'd begun to wonder how I was going to cope with the physical exertion of labor after weeks and weeks in bed. But part of me is horrified. My sister gave birth normally, with a great deal of determination and a stiff upper lip. She bore her children like a healthy animal, without help or intervention. Just like my mother—"Who are these women 'too posh to push'?" I remember her saying at Alison's bedside. "I don't know what the world's coming to, in my day we just got on with it, a bit of pain never hurt anyone. Alison knows that, she's got backbone this one." Alison, pale and spent, smiled back at her, then over at me, with the smugness of a woman whose mettle had been tested and proven. "It was hard, Mummy, but it was worth it," she said, virtuously. **I may be daughter number two,** she telegraphed at me, **but I'm gaining ground.**

I'll lie passive and supine and be handed my child by a surgeon. I can't seem to do any part of this baby thing right.

After the appointment I perched on a low iron railing, breathless from the exertion of walking down Dr. Weinberg's corridor, while Tom hailed me a cab. "Why is this happening to us?" I heard him mutter, half under his breath; "I just can't deal with—ah. Come on, Q," he called, in a louder voice, as a long yellow taxi pulled up, and he came over, grabbed me under the arm, and pulled me up. "I have to get back to the office, I've got meetings all afternoon. I'll probably be home after you've gone to bed, so don't wait up." "As **if**," I replied coldly, heaving my awkward figure into the backseat without a backward glance.

He slammed the door shut without another word and set off along the sidewalk.

A few moments later we drove past him— long raincoat swinging, head down, staring at the ground. The lights were green, the driver accelerated; I watched my husband's figure as it receded into the distance, that well-loved gait, the curly hair I used to trim in the mornings, when both of us were naked and giggling, neat at the nape of his neck, longer at the crown, cropped at the sides. And as I craned to look back at him through the corner, the left-most tip-top edge of the window, a tiny shape now almost lost in the crowds, I thought I saw (or was it only in my mind's eye?) a tall blond woman in a red suit, double-taking, looking back at him over her shoulder. I thought to myself, any woman would think, as I once did, My God, **there's** a good-looking man—affluent, desirable, respectable, I wonder if he's available…

I sighed and slumped back in the seat. A few moments later I caught myself grinding my teeth, and when the cab lurched to a stop at a red light, I clenched my hands so hard around the safety strap that I opened the cut on my finger again. A drop of blood slipped from the tip and fell onto the sill of the cab's window. Like something out of a fairy tale—"Snow White" perhaps, or "Sleeping Beauty." Maybe I'm about to produce a child with skin as white as snow and lips as red as blood. Or maybe I'll fall into an enchanted sleep, separated from my family and everyone I love, that lasts for a hundred years.

Oh, I forgot, that bit's already happened.

48

Lottie, an old friend of mine from London, recently sent us a fairy-tale anthology, a huge tome with galloping blue-eyed girls and crouched green trolls on the cover. "Here's to many happy years of bedtime stories," she wrote in sprawling blue pen on the flyleaf. I loved fairy tales when I was little. When you're a child, you're constantly figuring out the boundary between the real and the unreal. You're not quite sure whether demons and fairies exist or not, whether a fat man comes down your chimney with a big sack of presents at Christmas, whether your parents are actually witches in disguise. Fairy tales are helpful because they literalize all that stuff. People turn into animals at the drop of a hat. Wolves lurk in dark places with red eyes, slavering tongues, and an epicurean preference for small children. But these last few days I've been rereading the tales and wondering about the lessons kids learn at the **end**. Everything seems to wind up great for the good people—the princes and princesses get married, and the evil beasties meet with a hideous blood-curdling death. I suppose that's all kids can cope with, but it's hardly an accurate representation of life, is it? We teach our children that everything works out for the best if they're good and well behaved, but all the time we know it's not true. Bad things happen to us no matter what. Princes and princesses may love each other ever so much—so much it hurts—but it doesn't mean they're going to live happily ever after.

49

Friday 1 P.M.

My stomach is scored with purplish stretch marks. I seem to have developed half-a-dozen in the last twenty-four hours. I am torn between horror at the sight of my scarred skin and a feeling of satisfaction and relief; after all, stretch marks are an outward sign of the baby's development. He **must** be all right if he's growing so fast.

Lara came to visit me this morning, after breakfast. I rolled my eyes when I first heard her call my name outside the door, but then I heard a strange catch in her voice as she said, "Q, is it okay if I come in?"

One glance at her face was all I needed to confirm the dawning suspicion; it was immediately obvious that she had found out about Mark's affair. New lines were sharply etched around her mouth.

"I'm in trouble, Q," she said to me as she hovered uncertainly in the middle of the sitting room. "I don't know what to do."

Sit down, I told her, and she subsided into our leather armchair without taking off her long belted couture coat. She sat, huddled, with her hands deep in her pockets, staring at the floor.

Lara is an irritating and self-obsessed woman, but I couldn't help feeling for her. She looked terrible. Her hair is usually gathered up into a high, jaunty ponytail; today it was lank and unwashed, and three-quarters of it had escaped its silver clip and hung limply around her face. Her skin had that slack, used look that women get when they haven't slept properly and are no longer in their teens. Her fingernails were bitten, her tan stockings loose and wrinkled about the knees. She looked as if someone had started to disassemble her.

I took all of this in while she sat, silent, a ghastly contrast to the last time I saw her. After a few moments of silence she swallowed hard, then said into the kilim, "Mark told me last night he's leaving me for another woman."

I debated my response, but suddenly it struck me that she didn't give a damn what I said or didn't say. She was too wrapped up in her pain.

She passed her hands wearily over her eyes. "Apparently he's been having an affair for the best part of a year, and now he—wants to start over, with this new girl. I—oh God, you must be wondering why I'm here telling you this. But I was sort of hoping you, or Tom, might be able to talk to him, maybe persuade him not to leave me...?" The question mark hovered in the air between us.

Oh good God, I thought.

I don't have any influence on Mark, I told her at last, but I will talk to him, if you like. And I can ask Tom to talk to him too, only—only I don't know if he will, I finished lamely. She nodded helplessly. "I don't expect it to work, but I have to try everything," she said. "**Everything**. He told me he was spending last night at a hotel," she added, with a bitter laugh. "But I'm sure he was with **her,**" she finished, as if strangely forced into the humiliating confession, into opening the wound and exposing it to my gaze. "The kids asked me what was happening, I said he was on a business trip. I don't know how I'm going to tell them he's not coming home." Her voice broke into a hundred jagged shards.

I sat and watched her cry. There was nothing else I could do.

Finally, she gave a sort of choking gasp and stood up, wiping her nose hurriedly on her cuff. "I'm sorry about this, Q. The last thing you need, I'm sure," she said, a sickly smile on her lips. "You're a good friend. We girls stick together, don't we?"

I smiled falsely back at her, feeling terrible. Of course I didn't tell her I was already best friends with her husband's mistress. Or that I was inadvertently the means of reuniting her husband with his lover. How could I?

5 P.M.

I was brooding over Lara's visit when Mummy called in high excitement, to say she's bought her plane ticket ("I used the **Internet,** dear. It's rather amazing. You can buy all sorts of things. And it's much cheaper than Johnson's on the high street, did you know?"). She has also bought herself a new wardrobe (she either thinks we don't have clothes in America or believes we require a certain level of sartorial elegance from our visitors, I'm not sure which). And she has purchased an extraordinary array of guidebooks and swears she wants to "do the sights" ("I've written down where I want to go, where is it, oh here it is, in this little folder with color-coded sections, it's under 'blue,' now listen dear and tell me if you think I've covered everything, empirestate-

buildingstatenislandferryellisislandgrandcen-
tralcentralparkchryslerbuildingtheworldtradec
entersitemomawhitneythemetropolitanmuseu-
mofartnewyorkpubliclibrarytimessquaresohow-
estvillageupperwestsideharlemqueensbrooklyn-
thebronx…").

"And perhaps, dear," she continued, excit-
edly, "once you're up and about a bit, we can go
farther afield." She paused. "I've always wanted
to see **Maine**. Can we go to Maine, do you think,
dear?"

I gulped. I didn't want to throw cold water on
this unexpected enthusiasm, but—**Maine**? "It's
quite **far,** Mummy," I said, faintly. "It would take
us six or seven hours to get there, and I'm not
sure what the baby will think of the drive…"

"As much as that, you think?" she said, sounding discouraged, and then, with returning confidence, "No, I don't think you can be right, dear, I
think it's a good deal closer than that."

"No, Mummy, really—"

"I'm quite sure it's closer," she said firmly,
with the air of one who would simply move it
closer if worst came to worst. "Two hours should
do it. Let's pencil in Maine, anyway, and if we
have a spare day we'll tootle up the coast and
have lunch, there's a jolly good place listed in my
guidebook…"

So I can only assume she's looking forward
to her visit, although her anxieties have not com-

pletely disappeared. She told me she's bought a pair of compression stockings to guard against thrombosis of the leg on the flight, and a mask in case the person sitting next to her appears to have the flu ("Well, dear, it might not be **English** flu!" she said, in vaguely outraged tones. "It might be the one those poor people in China have, and there's also a bird one isn't there, really you can't be too careful these days…"). She also has a money belt for her "valuables" (the mind veritably boggles, because her wedding ring is Mexican silver and her watch is a battered Timex with a frayed cloth band) and finally (this is my favorite) a pepper spray to fend off attackers. "It's also a foghorn, and a torch," she told me seriously, "and a radio. Really, it's very versatile."

50

Midnight

"There's something I need to discuss with you," Tom said to me a few hours ago as I sat by the sink on the wooden stool in our bathroom, brushing my teeth.

I took a deep breath. "Go on," I said quietly, thinking, **at last**. The moment has finally arrived.

Since he got back from Tucson and Baltimore he's spent an appalling amount of time in the office, but even when he's here he's treated me with a terrifying, aching politeness. I don't know how to talk to him when he's like this. I don't even know where to begin. He's like an opaque window, a closed vault, a sealed letter.

He leaned his butt against the vanity, crossed his legs, then his arms, and stared into the middle distance. I heard his breathing turn shallow. "Q, a while back, in the hospital, you asked me to quit Crimpson. Then there was that other stupid fight, before I left...I've been thinking a lot about everything you said, and you have to know—I'm not prepared to do it. To quit, I mean. Making partner at Crimpson—it's the most important thing in my life. And realizing that—realizing that..." He paused. The world paused—

"Realizing that has made me see that—that—"

"I'm **not**," someone said, and I realized from the peppermint froth bubbling down my chin that it was me.

I put down the brush and reached for the soft green hand towel looped through a ring on the wall. Then I wiped my mouth. There was a strange sound in my ears, as if a huge curtain was being ripped in two.

It took a while for me to notice that Tom was still speaking. I couldn't hear what he was saying, but I saw his lips moving in the oval beveled mirror on the opposite wall. I don't know what you're saying, I told him. I don't hear you. You'll have to say it all again, I'm afraid, because I think I need to know if you're going to leave me.

He turned and looked at me, and I noticed that his eyes were full of tears. His eyes are the color of the soap in the dish, the tiles on the wall, the door to the shower, sea green, blue-green, my favorite color. "Leave you—Christ, I—Q, that's not what I mean, at least—I don't know what I'm going to do. I just know that I can't settle for some second-class job at some third-tier firm. Because you and I both know I can't go to any old job. The hours aren't going to be much better unless I take a big jump down the ladder. You may be happy with that, but I know I won't be. At Crimpson I deal with huge clients and big issues. I'm not willing to spend my life dealing with the same five zoning issues month in and month out. I can't do it, Q, I'm sorry. Where does that leave us?"

I don't know, I said, wearily. Slowly I stood up. Then—because I couldn't think what else to do—I turned my back on him and, leaving him alone in the bathroom, crept into bed like an animal into its hole.

Tom stood in the doorway to the bathroom, looking at me, his face a mix of concern and frustration. I pulled the covers over my head and closed my eyes in the hot, suffocating darkness.

"Q, listen to me please." He seemed far, far away. I lifted the edge of the comforter slightly. "I can't lie to you, it's always been **us,**you and me, y'know? We've always been straight with each other. I can't pretend to you I'll be happy in a different job, now, can I?"

I thought about this. It sounded plausible, but there was some flaw in the argument. Oh yes, we're about to have a baby.

"We're about to have a baby," I said, my voice muffled by the comforter. I lifted it a couple of inches higher to watch the effect of my words.

"I know that," he said, impatiently, and started pacing up and down. "I know that, of course I do, but that doesn't mean our life has to stop, does it? That doesn't mean we have to give up everything that's important to us, right? And anyway, at the beginning, the baby will hardly know I'm around, I don't see it's going to make a big difference if I'm here in the evenings or not—"

"Right, but I take it you think **I** will be?" I said, furiously, struggling to sit up at last, fighting my way out of the heavy covers, "unless you think that the baby will be happy if **neither** of us is at home?"

"I don't see what you mean," he replied, bewildered. "Look, to be honest, I don't really know what this is all about, where it's come from. We agreed we'd get child care, a nanny. That's what we always said, so yeah, maybe we'll both be at work—"

"All day, every day, we'll both be at work, we'll never see this baby, is that what you think? After all this, after carrying him every day for nine months, lying in bed for three of them, you think I'm just going to walk out that door and leave him with some stranger from dawn to midnight? Is that what you think?" I yelled, picking up a pillow and throwing it at his face for added emphasis. "Is that what you think?"

"Well, yes," he said, catching the pillow calmly and laying it on the end of the bed. "That's exactly what I think. It's what people do."

"**No, it's not, it's not what people do,**" I shouted, so hard my throat hurt. My larynx seemed to be closing, my voice sounded strangled and hoarse, it was like someone else's voice, not mine at all. "It's not what people do, or if it is, it's horrible, kids want to see their parents, this isn't a mother-kid thing, this is a **parent**-kid thing, do you understand? I don't care what we said or didn't say all those months ago, it doesn't matter now, everything's changed, can't you see that? We're having a baby, Tom, please, try to understand..." My voice failed me, and I started to cry, weakly, pathetically. Why do the tears come just when we most want to seem cool and collected? But the pregnancy hormones descended like a huge wet web, sticky and suffocating and inescapable. I tried to claw it away but I couldn't, the sobs were deep inside my solar plexus now, the web was over my face, I could hardly breathe.

My husband stood and watched me, his weary eyes tense and shadowed.

"Q, I don't think you're thinking straight," he said at last. "If you're considering quitting Schuster and staying home I guess that's something we can discuss, although I'm not convinced it's what you really want. But as for me—look, I have plenty of colleagues with kids, they just manage somehow, I'm not saying it's ideal, but they survive. They put in quality time when they can, and they hope their kids will understand. They make it up to them, and their wives, later, when they've reached the top of the profession. And that's what I'm going to do. Because I'm determined to make partner at Crimpson. I don't want to upset you, Q, but we have to get this straight; I'm not going to quit." He turned and walked out of the bedroom.

I watched Oprah this afternoon, the topic was "building a marriage for a lifetime." The consensus of the guests (sitting with hands discreetly propped on the spousal knee, the women in looped beads and hand-knit sweaters, the men in uncomfortable trousers) was, don't forget the romance. Help me, Oprah, please, because I fear it's going to take more than a candelabra and a filmy negligee to get my relationship back on track.

51

Saturday 8:30 A.M.

I stumbled into the kitchen an hour ago to find a note propped up against the saltcellar. For a terrible moment I thought, that's it, he's left me for good. **Dear Q, I choose my job, raise the kid on your own, damn you.** But the note simply said that he may have to work through the night tonight and asked me (as an afterthought) to call if I needed anything.

Needless to say, I won't.
Crack open Sylvia Plath's **Ariel** when life seems too hard to bear. It's always good to discover that someone else has been closer to the screaming edge than you are.

11 P.M.

Tom can barely bring himself to look at me, but five minutes ago he arrived home unexpectedly with a large citron tart, which he deposited on the table beside the sofa. Then he vanished into the bathroom to take a quick shower and change his clothes, telling me, tersely, that he's going back to the office in half an hour.

I'm not sure what to make of the gesture (although I **do** know what to do with the tart itself, I've already shoveled about half of it into my mouth, and it's incredible. The pastry's light and crumbly, the fat melts in the mouth, the lemon fizzes and zings on the tongue). What does it mean? Is the cake in place of his love?

It certainly doesn't seem to augur a change of heart on his part, a renewal of intimacy with a bed-bound Q. He dumped the tart heavily beside me, dropped his briefcase by the sofa, then stomped off into the bedroom with a closed face.

I stared at the briefcase resentfully. Rectangular, hard sides, dark maroon, with bright bronze locks. Always in his arms, always by his side, a present from his father to celebrate the job at Crimpson ("Not a bad little job, son, not a bad job at all. It's not brain surgery, though is it, haha!"). I hate that briefcase, always have, nothing soft about it, a constant reminder of Peter's excessively high standards, his cold superiority, and the condescending way he treats **me,** as if he's thinking, She's just a girl, she'll trip up at some point, realize the significance of her uterus, and get back into the kitchen where she belongs. (Some men seem to undress you with their eyes; Peter always seems to take off my skin. Whenever he's looking at me I have the distinctly uncomfortable feeling he's stripping off my epidermis and peeking at my innards, reaching in and handling them, heart and womb and liver, inspecting them to see if they're functioning according to his exacting standards. A most unpleasant feeling.)

Then a terrible thought came to me. Tom is working for the enemy, in a sense **he's** the enemy now. What's to stop me from **opening his briefcase** (I know the combination) and rifling through it for Randalls-related documents? For something—let's say—that proves the black mold story is just a way for Randalls to get out of its obligations to its rent-controlled tenants?

For a moment I paused, electrified; I listened to the sound of the shower running in the distance and thought, I could do it right now, I have five minutes at least before he comes back...But, of course, I didn't. It would be absolutely unethical for me as a lawyer. And there may not be a clause about this in the marriage ceremony, but it's basically implicit: don't betray your husband. Under any circumstances. In sickness or in health.

52

Monday 2 P.M.

But there are other ways to pursue my ends. I've spent the morning drafting an account of Randalls's iniquities, which I'll recommend that Fay send to the **New York Times**. And a few local TV stations as well. "Randalls is applying to demolish the present 1940s construction, which currently houses a thriving Greek community, and replace it with a yuppie-pleasing thirty-story apartment block. Randalls's legal representatives, Smyth and Westlon and Crimpson Thwaite (the latter currently have one of the largest real estate practices in New York) are either incompetently unaware of their client's unethical behavior or culpably supporting attempts to purge the building by giving tenants false information..." That should do it. They can take pictures of Mrs. G and her friends outside the building looking noble but woebegone, the real face of New York City, hardworking immigrants who deserve the opportunity to enjoy the quiet time of life.

My mother arrives tomorrow afternoon. Of course she'll think Randalls's shenanigans are only par for the course in a place like New York City. She probably thinks most landlords bury their recalcitrant tenants beneath the tarmac of the nearest Interstate.

3 P.M.

Christ, I've just had a phone call from Lucille, Tom's mother. Turns out Peter is in the city attending a conference today, Lucille's come up with him from Baltimore, and they want to have dinner with us here this evening. That's all I need. A surfeit of parents.

I haven't seen Lucille in a year. (We caught up with Peter about five months ago, he had lunch with us after another of his surgeons' conferences. "Theo's delighted to hear you've got that wife of yours pregnant at last," he said to his son jovially, referring to a school friend of Tom's, and I choked angrily on the soup. "Got me pregnant"? As if conceiving for a woman is all about lying supine while your husband pokes his semen into your belly.) Lucille's voice was, as always, thin and nasal on the phone, with that faint Bostonian twang, the extra **w**'s that seem to invade the spaces between consonants and vowels. "We've felt so bad for not seeing you these past few months," she said, calmly. "But Tom said there was nothing we could do for you, and we've been terribly busy." Mmmm, I said, I'm sure you have. Tom told me all about the choral society concert, it sounds **exhausting**.

It was, she said, sounding vaguely suspicious, although that's not what I meant. I'm sure you know Peter's been writing a book on modern heart transplant procedures. I've been working with him on the edits, which was quite a performance. The publisher wanted him to cut about ten thousand words, but they were all such good words; I felt he shouldn't excise a single one. Still, they were absolutely insistent…

I switched off and peered at my toenails, which I can now only glimpse if I kick my feet and twist my head at the same time. They need cutting, but it looks as if they'll have to wait until after the birth. **("He's so talented, he has such a gift for prose, so clear yet so elegant...")**

Unless—presumably you can get a pedicure in your home? I reached, with some difficulty, for the phone book on the bottom shelf of the side table.

P for Pedicurists. No, that's not right. It's terribly hard to use the yellow pages in a culture that's not your own; it's almost impossible to intuit how another country organizes itself. "Cinemas" are "Movie Theaters" in the States, cars are "Automobiles," and the Brit who attempts to find the nearest "Garage" for a tune-up will draw a blank. And don't try to use the automated telephone services because the robotic woman on the other end of the phone won't be able to understand your accent. I often find myself affecting a fake American drawl to placate her. Wait, here we are, pedicures under "Personal Care and Services." In the comfort of your own home. Maybe I'll get a manicure as well. And a haircut! That's a good idea, I haven't had one in months. And what about a massage?

Meanwhile Lucille's still talking (**"his colleagues say they've never met a man with**

such a gift for communication, such command of the English language…").

So the pair of them will be here to drive me nuts in three hours, but at least I have a week's worth of luxurious body-care lined up in my diary. Tom swears he'll get out of work for a few hours so he can be here when his parents arrive; if you think I'm entertaining those two on my own (I said), you've got another thing coming. I'm not opening the door, which means that if you're not home by six, your parents will be spending a great deal of time in the hallway this evening. You understand?

9 P.M.

"My dear," Lucille whispered to me over coffee, confidentially, "Tom tells me you're thinking of giving up work, is this true?"

I glanced up at her, then over at Tom, who was pouring his father a large glass of scotch on the rocks and didn't appear to have heard. "I—we're thinking about what to do when the baby's born, yes," I said, unwillingly.

Lucille nodded, her pearl drop earrings clicking faintly somewhere within her curled and perfumed hair. "Of course you are, my dear," she said, briskly. "It was always obvious to me—to us—that you'd have to give it up when the little one is born." She reached forward suddenly and touched my belly with a smug, possessive smile that made me want to scream. I flinched, but she didn't seem to notice. Her hand stayed on my navel, sickly warm, encroaching, white and slack and covered in gemstones, a rich old woman's hand.

"You have to put him first," she said, serenely. "It's what a mother does."

"Tom may leave Crimpson," I said suddenly, I don't know why, but my husband heard this time all right. "**What?**" gasped Peter. "**What?**" gasped Lucille. Their words, their shock, hung in the air, vivid as a red balloon. All three of them stared at me, three mouths open, three pairs of eyes wide, holes, lots of holes in lots of white faces, but I couldn't see inside any of them—

"Yes," I gabbled, "he may leave Crimpson because of the hours, because he wants to spend more time with his son. You're right, Lucille"—I moved her hand off my belly, but she hardly noticed—"we have to put **him** first now. So Tom's seriously thinking about leaving his firm and trying to find something less exhausting, something less—" I stopped.

Tom was the first to speak. He put down his glass slowly on the table and turned to face his father. "We have been thinking seriously about all sorts of life changes," he said to Peter, levelly, neutrally, the skin around his eyes white and taut, "including the possibility that I might leave Crimpson. We think, on balance, that this is **not** the best idea"—there was an audible outtake of breath in the room—"but Q sweetly wants me to be sure. She doesn't want me to stay in a job for the money. I've really appreciated her support on this," he added, turning to me, his blue eyes virtually black, like the sky before a violent storm. "I can always trust her to support me. Always."

We held each other's gaze for about two seconds, then both looked away at precisely the same moment. Peter was nodding sagely. "It's good to think things through, son," he said seriously, "although the last thing you want to do when a child comes is lose the bulk of your income"—as though my salary was mere pin money, a few hundred toward the dry-cleaning bill. "And children need someone to look up to," he added, warming to the theme. "They want a strong father figure, boys especially." He then clapped Tom's shoulder. "Not that you need my advice, but if you **were** to ask me"—he lifts his lip in the semblance of a smile, exposing his pointy too-white teeth—"I'd tell you to stay on the treadmill, keep on with the good work, and your son will thank you for it when he's got the best education the city has to offer and a father he can be really proud of. You understand?"

Tom nodded.

I opened my mouth and screamed and screamed, although it seems I didn't, because the three of them just sat sipping their after-dinner drinks as if nothing untoward was happening at all.

53

Tuesday 10 P.M.

I perched illicitly (and precariously) on the window bench for twenty minutes earlier this evening and watched the sun set, the oranges and yellows ceding slowly to greens and blues. There's a lightness in the sky even now, an azure gleam that confirms the passing of the year. It may even be warm outside. People seem to be wearing sweaters and cardigans instead of overcoats. And they're walking more slowly now, no longer scurrying, rushing along the streets, but sauntering, strolling, hand in hand, shoulders pushed back, arms swinging, faces lifted to the sky.

In here it still feels cold—in more ways than one.

I was bundled up in my robe and the blue-and-gray wool blanket, leafing through this month's copy of **Vogue** for about the seventh time, when Tom came home. He dropped his briefcase by the door and produced, from a tall paper bag, a brand-new bottle of scotch. He twisted off the lid and poured himself a large tumblerful, which he drained. Then he poured himself another and turned to face me.

I saw Mark this evening, he said, his face inscrutable. We had a drink after work. He told me that he came to see you earlier this week to talk about his **affair**. Why didn't you mention it to me, Q? Don't you think I might've been just a **teensy** bit interested? He assumed I must know all about it, he's been waiting to hear from me all week—Christ! Why did you keep something so important from me, Q? What in God's name were you **thinking**?

I'd been watching him in silence ever since he walked into the apartment, wondering what was going through his mind. I'd prepared withering put-downs on a number of subjects, but unfortunately not on this one.

I rolled my eyes, feeling like a naughty teenager. Because I hardly see you these days, I said (even **I** thought I sounded childish, whiny, shrill). You get up when I'm still asleep, you arrive home after I've gone to bed. When, precisely, do you expect me to tell you things? Things of—any kind at all?

That's not fair, he replied, angrily; there **have** been opportunities. I admit I've been working very hard—let's not open up **that** subject again—but there have been times you could've talked to me. So again, Q, I'm asking you, why didn't you tell me?

I was about to snap back something about how he had no right to interrogate me like this, and would he like to shine a light in my eyes and stick pins under my fingernails—when it struck me: what **is** the answer to the question? Why **didn't** I tell him about Mark and Lara? Probably because I'd gotten into the habit of keeping things from you, I told him mentally, deliberately keeping my expression bland, unreadable. Because I don't **choose** to tell you what's going on in my life anymore.

"You've been plotting to get Mark together with that girl who's been hanging around here the past two months, haven't you?" Tom said at last, his voice low with barely repressed fury.

"What did you say?" I asked, taken aback. "With—with **Brianna**? Are you **serious**? Didn't Mark tell you I basically threw him out of the apartment when he asked for my help to get her back?"

"Oh sure—he said you were in a terrible mood, started swearing at him when he tried to tell you how bad he feels about Lara. You didn't want to hear **that,** did you? You've been trying to get him to leave her all along," he went on, coming to stand by the sofa and looking down at me.

I felt the magazine drop out of my nerveless fingers and onto the floor. Tom took another swig of whiskey.

"You know," he continued, breath reeking of fire and peat, "I've been wondering all evening why you'd do this. Were you just bored, did you want to feel important, was this your way to feel at the center of things? Or did you want to net a husband for your dimwit friend? Or—and Q, I'm **really** hoping it wasn't this—was this some weird, fucked-up plan to get back at me? Did you want to turn my best friend's life upside down by getting him to leave his wife for a bonehead who dresses like a hooker? Well, congratulations, Q. Whatever it is you wanted, I guess you've succeeded. But if I were you, I'd butt out of other people's lives, bed rest or no bed rest. And as for meddling in my friends' affairs to get at me—" He covered his face with his hands for a brief, appalling moment, then turned round and walked out of the room.

I was left staring speechlessly after him.

I've always loved Jane Austen novels, but I find the characters' inability to communicate with one another incredibly irritating. Elizabeth, for God's sake, tell Darcy you've changed your mind! Jane, go and ring on Bingley's door and let him know that you really care! My life lacks the subtlety of a Jane Austen novel, not to mention the pretty frocks and cotillion balls, but I feel I'm inhabiting her world all the same. I don't know how my husband feels, and I don't know how to explain the way **I** feel either. I can't begin to find the words.

And so I fold my lips together when he accuses me and say nothing at all.

A few moments later I discovered, to my shock, on the side table, a large beribboned box from the Bouley Bakery. I never even saw him put it down. Nestled inside were three banana and rum tarts, four cassis tarts, and a handful of Napoleons in pale rustling tissue paper. I stared at the box for about five minutes. What on earth does it **mean**?

54

Wednesday 11 A.M.

A delighted phone call from Brianna this morning. She spent the weekend with Mark, and it was "everything she'd ever dreamed of." They spent both mornings in bed, then wandered the streets of the city with their arms wrapped tight around each other, their bodies as close as they could manage. "And we were back in bed again by midafternoon, and **oh, Q**! I can't tell you..."

Don't try, I said sourly, but I don't think she noticed the tone. Mark is contacting his lawyer this week to start arranging the divorce from Lara. I made a halfhearted stab at suggesting they might like to wait a bit (Lara's haggard face lives on in my memory), but Brianna barely heard me, and it's not as if she'd take my advice even if she did.

I'll have to call Lara and ask her how she's coping—a phone call I'm not looking forward to making. I'll have to do it before my mother arrives in—oh, good God, she lands in a few hours. Even as I'm typing this the woman is hurtling toward me at five hundred miles an hour, propelled by four engines and a great deal of determination.

She's equipped with a detailed list of instructions on how to negotiate the airport and find herself a taxi. She expressed some suspicion about the ease of making it into the terminal building from the plane itself—"airports are terribly badly signposted," she announced grandly, with the air of one who was in Dubai just the other week—so I described every escalator, every moving stairway I could remember at JFK. Of course now I'm terrified that she'll end up on a plane to Reykjavik, although that mightn't be such a bad outcome. I suspect a land of thin sunshine and spurting geysers would be more to her taste than the close, dark, bisected streets of New York City.

4 P.M.

She is on her way. She just called to say she's in the taxi queue ("They really are yellow, dear, I thought that was just a Hollywood touch") and will be walking through the door in less than an hour. I called Tom to warn him—he expressed a vague suspicion (or was it hope) that she'd bottle at the last moment and claim an unexpected hole in her yoga schedule.

55

Thursday

"My dear girl, should you be eating **quite** so many tarts?"

"It's a sweet flat—'apartment' I suppose you call it—but rather small for my taste."

"Heavens, this orange juice has bits in it, if you tell me where you keep the sieve I'll strain it for you."

Meanwhile Tom and I are talking in neutral beige tones; our voices neither rise nor soften.

56

Friday 10 A.M.

Thank God, she's launched herself into the streets of Manhattan armed with a subway map and no fewer than five well-thumbed guidebooks. ("Mrs. Walberswick from the village Bowls club came to New York last year, and she wouldn't set foot outside her hotel without her nephew, since, let's face it, the city is a very dangerous place. But don't worry about me, I have my pepper spray, dear.") She'll be home by three, because I have another appointment with Dr. Weinberg at four.

I think she's having a nice time. I, meanwhile, am pondering the meaning and the usage of the verb "to defenestrate." I defenestrate my mother. My mother has been defenestrated. See! She is defenestrating.

Tom, to give him his due, has behaved impeccably so far. He's been listening with the appearance of profound interest while she's regaled us with "stories" about the flight—"and they gave us these little plastic pouches, wonderful really, I think I'll use mine for my dirty washing. Inside was a pair of earplugs and a little sachet of moisturizer, and an eye mask, not that I used mine, it had a pair of eyes marked on it, and I don't like to look silly while I sleep, who does? But there was also a pink plastic pen, which you can have if you like, dear, because you can never have too many pens, and the person next to me didn't take his, so I took a second one when we were 'deplaning.' I was a bit worried I was stealing, so I waited till the air hostess was looking the other way, but I don't think it was stealing really, was it, **was it**? Do you think it was stealing, dear?"

Tom assured her that he didn't think it was stealing and accepted the plastic pen with an air of sincere gratitude. So for the time being, at least, she's quite impressed with him.

Rather more impressed, to be frank, than she is with me. "My dear, you're putting on a great deal of weight," she told me seriously (as if I haven't looked in a mirror recently). "It can't be good for the baby, having such a lethargic mother. I wouldn't be surprised if you were putting yourself at risk for a heart attack. I think you need to streamline your diet, dear. Oh, it's a good thing I'm here. You need to eat more raw food, and especially more bean sprouts. Bean sprouts are remarkably good for you, did you know? I'll get you some today and a few packets of rice cakes as well."

My mother has all the zeal of the convert. Bean sprouts = good. Everything else = bad. Not that she is particularly imaginative about her food; the odd thing is, in spite of her yogic ardor, she has many of the prejudices of pre-1970s rural England (she still thinks pizza is a bit exotic). She peered at my list of possible lunch options yesterday with considerable suspicion and only brightened when (in some despair) I suggested a cheese-and-pickle sandwich. Bean sprouts seem to be her one great nod to modernity, and she's terribly impressed with herself for being so avant garde ("Mrs. Hutchinson won't eat them, isn't that ridiculous? I invited her over for dinner one day last week, and she walked round them, wouldn't try so much as a single sprout. But then your mother was always rather ahead of her generation, I'm sure you remember that I was the first one on the street to use nonbiological washing powder").

Both mornings she's vanished after breakfast to do her yoga practice in her room. She emerges with a cat-got-the-cream look of serenity on her face and a drip of sweat nuzzling her cheekbone. She's desperate for me to join her, but there's something very uncomfortable about being led in yoga by my mother—all that getting in touch with your body seems a bit sexual somehow. So I've made my excuses, although the truth is, I'm looking forward to my massage on Monday to help loosen up the sword-sharp tension in my shoulder blades.

Saturday 3 P.M.

I wonder what the chances are of my mother's getting out of this place alive? (They may be increased by the fact that I can't get to the kitchen knives.)

The lovely Alexis showed up after dinner yesterday evening; Tom wasn't home, and my mother somehow got it into her head that she had to defend my honor from Alexis's marauding intentions. So she refused to leave the room, this in spite of the fact that Alexis obviously wanted to talk to me about Brianna, **and** in spite of the fact that I am eight months pregnant with another man's child. But my bewildering mother watched him suspiciously over her copy of the **New York Times** Metro section with a visage that might have been appropriate if I was a nineteenth-century virgin and Alexis a Regency Buck. Poor Alexis obviously realized there was some kind of misunderstanding, but he couldn't quite figure out what it was. He kept stealing bemused half-glances at her, then at me, as if he couldn't decide what he was accused of. This, to be honest, was not flattering from my perspective. I don't think it even crossed his mind that my mother imagined he might have designs on me.

When he finally left, my mother folded her lips together, crossed her arms, and sighed significantly.

I said nothing. I picked up the Sports section of the **New York Times** and began to read about last night's defeat of the Knicks at the hands of the Cleveland Cavaliers.

My mother shook her head sadly, tried to catch my eye, and sighed heavily once more.

I stared at a photograph of Allan Houston and said nothing.

My mother tutted and did some more head shaking.

Still, I said nothing. The Cavs had scored 108 points, and LeBron James had a breakout game.

My mother said, "Oh dear, dear, **dear,**" then did some more head shaking and finally a bit more tutting in a full-on, pull-all-the-stops-out moment of passive aggressivness that served her purpose.

"**What?**" I said, ten decibels louder than necessary, throwing down the newspaper with an expressive rustle.

"Don't shout, dear," my mother said mildly. "There's no need. I'm right opposite you."

"For Christ's sake, if you have something to say, then say it," I said hotly.

"Well, dear, if you don't mind me saying so, do you really think you should be entertaining young men in your husband's absence at night? This is New York, after all."

Mother, I told her, young men are as able to restrain their passions in New York as anywhere else in the world. And Tom knows perfectly well there's nothing going on with Alexis—

"Are you **sure** he knows that, dear?" she said, seriously, "because I think there's a weeny bit of tension between the two of you. I may be stepping out of line here, but still…"

I was hardly going to tell her the real substance of the tension between us, and frankly I'd be damned if I was going to admit there was any tension at all, so we passive-aggressived ourselves silly until Tom came home.

It was our second major argument. I'd already gotten mad at her for treating Dr. Weinberg like a witch doctor and the doorman—well, like a doorman.

So far today, we've behaved toward each other with a courtly politeness more appropriate to a couple of Arthurian knights than a twenty-first-century mother and daughter ("Would you like some tea?" "Oh yes please, how very kind of you, I would love some tea, would you like the Travel section of the paper?" Oh yes please...").

This morning she went baby shopping—leaving me to stare glassily at **Ricki** repeats—and came back with something she called, rather endearingly, a "lafayette." The clothes are useful enough and nice quality, which helped make the peace. At the moment she's in the basement of the building washing all of the baby-wear so it's ready for use. I'll restrain my murderous intentions for now.

57

Monday Midday

I'm thirty-five weeks pregnant today, a huge milestone, a day I've been dreaming of for nine long weeks. If the baby was born right now, he might be able to come home from the hospital with me. His lungs may be mature already, and he's already close to a normal birthweight. At my appointment last week the sonographer estimated that he was about five pounds.

Last weekend was quiet, if hardly tension free. I folded the baby clothes; my mother put the sheets on the bassinet and charitably rearranged the furniture in her room to make it as nursery-like as possible. She hung new curtains and blackout blinds on the window, then moved the single bed against the wall, next to the changing table, and put the crib in the middle of the room. On Sunday she bought some crates shaped like train carriages for toy storage. She struggled home with them on the subway, three piled high in her arms, then filled them with a suitcaseful of new toys—cuddly bears, board books, brightly colored rattles, plastic teething rings.

I went to see Dr. Weinberg this morning, and then Cherise in her dark, womblike room. Today's ultrasound showed that the baby is still breech—not that I needed someone to tell me that a very hard skull is lodged underneath my ribs—and therefore still needs to be delivered by C-section. But my fluid level is stable, so Weinberg has decided to shoot for thirty-seven weeks ("Just a bit further, yes? The pregnancy's going a little better now, I think we can get that far"), by which time the baby will technically be full term. In the meantime she wants to see me three times a week.

My mother held my hand very tightly while Dr. Weinberg talked through the arrangements for the operation. I'm overwhelmed with emotions. I'm excited to know that I'll be holding my baby so soon, but I'm also terrified because, truthfully, I have no idea how involved Tom is going to be. Some days I catch him watching me with a look in which love—naked, transparent love—and wistfulness are fused; on others, I think he's on the edge of leaving me, so close that a moth's breath might push him over. So while I'm horrified at the thought that my mother will be here for weeks to come ("I think I can get more cover at the studio, Q, then I can stay for another week or so and help you when the baby is born"), I'm also relieved that she's here in case I wake up one morning and find a second, final note propped against the saltcellar on the kitchen table.

But even supposing—or assuming—Tom is still here, I know that I'm going to need my mother's help. Because, frankly, I have no idea how to look after a baby. I'm convinced that I'm going to break him somehow. The newborns I've seen have necks that snap terrifyingly backward whenever you so much as nudge them. And how do you change a nappy? I've studied the diagrams in **Yes! You're Having a Baby,** but the children in those pictures seem suspiciously cooperative to me. I can't imagine the kicky creature I have inside me staring peaceably at the ceiling while I mop his bits. And that's another worry. Should I hold it when I clean him or will that send him into twenty years of psychoanalysis?

5 P.M.

Lulu, my therapeutic masseur, tells me that I have a lot of tension in my neck—and my upper back, my lower back, my shoulder blades, my sacrum, my cranium, my glutes, my...after one hour and $200 I feel about—ooh, 1 percent better. A day of continuous massaging (with perhaps some naked sybarites oiling my feet and waving palm fronds in my face) and I might start to unwind.

58

Tuesday 10 A.M.

A phone call from Jeanie this morning, just after breakfast. My mother was out searching for a particular brand of pacifier ("dummy," as we call them in England, I'm not sure which is worse) when the phone rang. "How's it going, Q love? Still on talking terms with Mummy dearest?" she asked, cheerfully.

Just about, I told her. She's driving me up the wall, but we're managing.

Then Jeanie told me about some football match that Dave played over the weekend. Apparently he's involved in a local youth action program to help troubled kids. The program organizes trips to amusement parks, beaches, and so forth, and it also has its own football league. This weekend saw a particularly successful match between two groups of kids representing twelve burglaries, fifteen narcotics infractions, and three possessions of unauthorized weapons. I listened to her glowing account of the children's improved manners and raised school grades for about ten minutes, with Alison's parting words sounding in my ears.

It was clearly time to speak. I took a deep breath.

Jeanie, I have to apologize. I may have been a bit hasty, I told her at last (with teeth only slightly gritted). Perhaps I judged Dave too quickly, and I'm sorry.

There was a long pause.

Q, I'm worried about you, Jeanie returned, in accents of astonishment. One week alone with our mother and you've lost your spirit! Why aren't you telling me that Dave is a repugnant slimy slug? Why aren't you enumerating his financial failings? Why aren't you hectoring me on my appalling track record in the romance department?

I winced, several times. Mother has nothing to do with it, I told her; we haven't even talked about you and Dave. But Alison pointed out when she was here that—well, look, anyway, I'm sorry Jeanie, really sorry for—some—of the things I've said about Dave. Maybe this summer we can do that cottage thing in Cornwall, y'know? You can help me with the baby, it'd be a nice break.

I'd love to do that, she replied, still sounding as if she'd been knocked over the head with a large and heavy object. I'd really love it. And Q, when you get to know Dave, you'll see, he's not that bad.

"Not that bad" isn't exactly a ringing endorsement, but I didn't say anything. "If you like him, Jeanie, I'm sure he's a nice guy," I said untruthfully.

When my mother came home I told her about my conversation with Jeanie and its outcome. "Oh I'm glad to hear that," she said vaguely as she struggled to stretch a freshly washed cover over the baby's "ocean bouncer" chair. "I leapt to some silly conclusions at the beginning, but you know, it turns out that Dave is quite a pleasant young man. He's very good to his mother, who has advanced Alzheimer's disease. He goes to see her at least once a week, even though she lives in Yorkshire, which is quite a trek you know. That's why he has such a problem holding down a job, which is why he keeps running out of money. I lent him a few hundred the other week, and he's already paid me back eighty pounds by working the night shift at the local supermarket, stacking shelves. Which he didn't have to do, as I told him, but he said he couldn't bear being in my debt. I do like to see that attitude in young people, don't you, dear? Now do you think I have this thing on right?"

So it seems that Dave is Mother Teresa in disguise, while I seem to be well on my way to earning my Cruella De Vil credentials.

59

Wednesday 3 P.M.

The ultrasound this morning showed another fluid level dip, which is upsetting. But maybe Cherise made a mistake? I don't think she was concentrating properly today—she had a fight with her mother last night, which I now know all about (I preferred it when she was silent and morose), and the baby's heart rate sounded good. He also looked wonderful, healthy and content; he was sucking his thumb, would you believe, tiny fingers curled up and around in a tight, balled little fist. So I think I'll just ignore today's reading.

60

Thursday 6 P.M.

Today my mother told me the most extraordinary story. She was chatting with one of our neighbors by the mail slots at lunchtime and learned that our building also had black mold!

The neighbor—I've never met her, but she apparently lives on the ground floor—told my mother that mold problems started in her apartment when a pipe burst three years ago. Our landlord paid to clean up the water damage, replacing carpets and so forth, but about a year later, when the wooden window frames began to flake, a construction company discovered greenish black stuff growing deep inside the walls. Randalls was slow to act, so the neighbor (good yuppie that she is) hired an independent assessor who found stachybotrys atra, as well as a few other less dangerous types of mold. The neighbor sent a copy of the findings to Randalls, together with the assessor's recommendations, which were that Randalls hires a company to effect a thorough and immediate cleanup.

At this point Randalls dutifully hired a mold removal contractor, and the neighbor reported to my mother that the problem seems to be fixed. In fact, this conversation all came about because the neighbor was defending our landlord; Mummy was grumbling about the size of our apartments and the magnitude of the rents, and the neighbor told her that we do well for Manhattan and that our landlord had an unusually strong sense of professional responsibility.

But as I listened to my mother's account it came to me: I bet this was how Randalls first dreamed up the mold story as a way to get rid of its troublesome rent-controlled tenants. It knew that the building opposite had also suffered burst water pipes; it knew the age of the building and its type of construction, and it suspected that the complex would also have mold—which indeed it did. But rather than simply working to fix the problem, as it did in our building, Randalls found a company that was willing to recommend demolition. Our building has only one or two rent-controlled units left, so it nets the owners a nice income. The complex opposite happens to be full of dear old ladies and gentlemen who are still paying $500 a month for apartments that are worth close to five times that amount. Miracle of miracles, when black mold shows up in the apartments opposite, nothing but demolition will do.

I debated concealing from my mother why her story interested me so much. This whole saga is, after all, grist for her mill, a real-life example of underhanded Manhattan wheelings and dealings. But then I thought, sod it, the woman deserves some praise. Mummy, I told her, when her story was done, this was good detective work. You've found out something very interesting indeed.

Have I dear? she said, brightening: What?

I took a deep breath and told her the whole yarn about Randalls, Mrs. G, and the elderly immigrants. She listened very attentively. Tsk, tsk, she muttered at the end of my narrative, shaking her head solemnly. Landlords are the same the world over. My friend Mrs. Ruskin's landlord took two months' rent out of her bank account—

"by accident," he said—and refused to give one of them back again. The very idea! You've got to stand up to these people, you know, Q. Would you like me to go down to the girl on the ground floor with a concealed tape recorder and get her to repeat the story?

I blinked at her. My mother the sleuth. If I didn't know better I'd think she'd been reading too many Raymond Chandler novels. I don't think that'll be necessary, I told her, faintly; presumably there are records detailing Randalls's first encounter with stachybotrys atra. The lawyers at Schuster can look into this. But because of you, they'll know where to look.

Now then, dear, don't hesitate to use me, she said, sounding a bit like a horse who's been told it can't clear a particularly appealing gate. Maybe those evil Randalls men will get to the girl downstairs and **pay her off**! I think I should go down right now and...

No, really, Mummy, I said firmly; it's fine. Fay can find someone to research this. But I'm really grateful to you, and my friend Mrs. Gianopoulou will be too.

My mother positively preened. "Well, I **am** pleased! If there's anything else I can do, you only have to ask," she added, smoothing her hair and smiling broadly. "I'm here to help!"

She's now in the kitchen cooking vegetable cobbler, which was one of my favorite meals as a child. The apartment is filled with the fragrance of vegetables, broth, and hearty cheese dumplings. By my side is a modest glass of merlot. "Don't be silly, dear," she said, when I protested as she splashed out the wine into a goblet. "I drank a glass a day when I was pregnant with all three of you, doesn't seem to have done you any harm. And you need a bit of stress relief, Q. You came out of that massage looking as if you'd been prodded with a knife and fork for an hour, not lulled into a state of peaceful serenity. That poor woman was almost in tears when she left. If you won't do yoga with me, you'll have to find another means of unwinding."

Concerns about my weight seem to have abated. I overheard her telling Tom to get me a cheese-cake this morning, "and I know she loves biscuits with chocolate chips in them, do you think you could find such a thing anywhere around here, dear?"

61

Friday 11 A.M.

Lara called early this morning to say that Mark has packed up all his clothes and moved out for good. Mark called half an hour later to give us his new address. He and Brianna have taken an apartment together in the East Village. I could hear Brianna giggling in the background; after a few minutes she grabbed the phone from him (I heard her say "**My** turn now, Marky!" followed by something that sounded suspiciously like "You'll pay for that later, my girl" and a lot more giggling). She described her new bedroom to me in great detail (something about a hole in the ceiling and her plans to stencil a pineapple over it, very tedious), then made her excuses: "I have to get up to go to work now, Q, so we'll talk later—oh Christ, Marky, look at the time, we're going to be late **again**—"

Lara is still in the marital home with two children and a swelling belly. I promised her that as soon as I'm up and about I'll come to see her. Not that she's been much of a Florence Nightingale to **me,** but still—I feel sorry for her.

My mother overheard my conversation with Lara and asked me what it was all about when I got off the phone; she listened to my account of Mark's desertion with a darkening face. "Poor, poor lamb," she said sorrowfully, when I was done. "If you tell me where she lives I'll go and see her, if you like. I know what it's like to be left with three children. I'll cook her and the kids a meal of vegetable cobbler."

I stared at her wordlessly for a moment. Who would have thought my mother could be so, well, **humane**? Lara will be pretty surprised to receive a Tupperware container of stewed vegetables and cheese dumplings—I don't think she eats anything that doesn't have the word **gourmet** in the title—but somehow I think she'll appreciate the delivery all the same. Vegetable cobbler is the most comforting food I know.

3 P.M.

Over lunch my mother brought up the subject of poor Lara again. She was balanced on the very edge of our leather armchair, a plate wobbling on her lap. "Who will sit with the poor woman during birth?" she asked as she picked the onions cautiously out of her pastrami sandwich. "She'll need someone to support her during labor, you know."

I shrugged as I embarked on my second turkey-and-cranberry sub. It was perfectly made, the baguette white and light and flaky, the berries sweet and firm until they popped in the mouth, releasing intense, thickly sweetened juice. "Maybe Mark, I don't know. Or perhaps she'll choose some girlfriend to act as a birth partner."

My mother looked serious. "You must ask her about this, Q. If she doesn't have a close friend, I want you to offer to partner her, okay?"

"Me? Mother, we're not particularly close," I explained. "Lara doesn't want me present when she has her legs in the air and blood spilling everywhere. She's the kind of woman who runs the taps if she has to use the bathroom when we're in the living room. She's not going to want me at her delivery, I promise you." I slurped my third banana smoothie dry.

My mother shook her head. "Q, I want you to offer to be with her, seriously. There's something very frightening about facing labor on your own. When your father walked out on me before you were born—yes, I know I've never told you this, but it happened—I was absolutely terrified. Those were the days when there was never any question of asking a friend or a parent to sit with you. I had nightmares about it for weeks; in the end I begged him to take me back, just so I'd have someone beside me to hold my hand. I found him in Clacton-on-Sea with a woman he'd met through the British Legion and told him I'd take him on any terms. Not, I have to tell you, that he was a great deal of use while I was giving birth, but at least I didn't have to see the sympathy in the nurses' eyes. I think that would have killed me."

I was completely floored. "Dad left you **before I was born**?" I asked her, astounded.

My mother half-looked at me, then looked away. "Yes," she said, embarrassed. "Then he left again just after Alison was born, and then one more time for about a week when Jeanie was six months old. That time you were old enough to understand, so I told you that he was on tour with his band. But I was terrified that he'd left for good; I couldn't think what I was going to say if he never came home again. Apparently, the woman he'd left with got bored quickly, because he arrived back with his tail between his legs long before you got suspicious. I was terribly relieved."

I had the strangest sensation of being on a pitching boat in a strong gale. "Why didn't I know any of this? Why didn't you ever tell us?"

My mother shrugged. "I thought it would make you feel insecure. I wanted to protect you as much as possible, make you feel that home was a safe and happy place. And I wanted you to love your father. That was so important to me, Q. To be honest with you, I needed him. I didn't want to do it all on my own. I had no illusions about how hard it would be."

I looked back over the landscape of my childhood and everything seemed suddenly subtly different. The lighting had changed, darkened. A longer shadow stretched out behind my father. Not that I ever thought he was perfect, but still—

"Does Alison know? What about Jeanie? And why are you telling me now?" I asked, at last.

"Your sisters—no, they don't know," my mother replied. "And I'm only telling you now because—well, there's no reason to keep it a secret anymore, is there?" She got up from the arm-chair, fetched the teapot from the kitchen, and poured herself another strong cup of Yorkshire tea. "There's plenty more in the pot, dear, if you'd like some—?"

But I don't entirely believe her. I don't think that's the only reason she told me about my father's desertions today. I caught her watching me and Tom together this morning, the way we dance around intimacy, the way we avoid each other's eyes, the tiny nags that catch, like fishhooks, on the skin ("Do you **have** to bang the door?" "Do you **have** to scatter crumbs around the floor?"). Is she telling me to repair the breach, to close the gap? What was that she said?—**"I needed him. I didn't want to do it all on my own. I had no illusions about how hard it would be."**

The problem is, **my** husband's not in Clacton-on-Sea, he's in a different universe.

7 P.M.

Just got back from another trip to Dr. Weinberg's. She told me to start trying something called "breech tilts," which are supposed to help persuade the baby to pivot on his own so I can deliver vaginally. ("I don't think it will work," Dr. Weinberg said, equably, "but there's no harm in trying, eh?") As far as I can tell breech tilts are designed to turn large pregnant women into sources of public hilarity. One version has me on the floor with my ass sticking up in the air. The other involves lying on the floor with my hips up while my husband ("or your mother, for that matter, husbands don't have to be there") speaks words to the baby that are designed to encourage him to find his own way out. Come along baby, turn around. Turn to face the world. The opening to the uterus is your entrance to the world. Face the world, baby. Turn around.

If this works I'll eat my own placenta.

Fluid level down again, but hopefully it means nothing. Cherise didn't seem particularly bothered, and as Dr. Weinberg explained, these readings are only an approximation. Plus if my stretch marks are anything to go by, the baby's growing at an astounding pace.

11 P.M.

Just read an article on the Internet that claimed stretch marks are a result of the mother's weight gain, rather than the baby's. Aaaaaaaargh.

62

Saturday 9 A.M.

Since breakfast, I've been doing fetal kick counts, the other bit of homework Dr. Weinberg assigned me yesterday. I'm supposed to count the number of times the baby moves in the hour after I eat, when the baby's most active. I'm supposed to count seven kicks, rolls, swooshes, or whatever, then stop. But what's the fun of that? I'm proud to say that my child has kicked and rolled and swooshed **forty-five times** in the last hour. I obviously have a professional sportsman in there.

Noon

Thirty-two kicks since I finished my last chocolate brownie. I will clearly be able to retire and live on my child's earnings as a footballer. I'll be one of those mothers in the front row with a megaphone and T-shirt emblazoned with her son's image.

7 P.M.

Oh my God, is he dead? I finished dinner fifty-eight minutes ago and I've only felt five kicks. What should I do? **What should I do?**

7:02 P.M.

Phew—two quick kicks came in just under the wire. But I'm still anxious. I think I'll have another cookie and see if that wakes him up a bit.

63

Monday 9 A.M.

I am having a baby in a week. A WEEK! IN ONE WEEK! OH GOOD GOD.
I AM COMPLETELY TERRIFIED.

64

Tuesday 7 A.M.

Tom left at 5:30 this morning, slamming the door viciously behind him.

I was heaving myself wearily onto the sofa a few hours later when the phone rang. "Hiya, Q, good morning," said a chirpy voice on the other end, "This is Leanne at Crimpson Thwaite." Ah yes, I thought to myself, Tom's too-charming secretary, the lovely Leanne, leggy Leanne, lissome Leanne, a woman I'd have to run out of town if it wasn't for her deep and unwavering commitment to the equally lovely Alyssa.

"Tom just called to say that he thinks he's left some paperwork behind, a couple of files, so I'm sending a courier over to pick them up at eight, will you be home?"

Will I be home? Now let me think—

"The courier has detailed instructions on how to find them, so this shouldn't inconvenience you at all, but I just wanted to let you know to expect him, have a nice day!" Click.

I looked around the room. Not on the radiator bench, not on the side table, not on the armchair— ah yes, over there, on the table by the entrance to the kitchen. A black box file and a slim navy envelope file, lying on top of yesterday's **Times** but beneath a pile of postbaby outfits (Transitional Wear as they're euphemistically termed, i.e., enormous knickers, capacious T-shirts, and bras with a staggeringly long list of letters on the label) that arrived yesterday afternoon. I stumbled over to get the files ready; not, of course, that I'm supposed to get out of bed, but I don't particularly want the courier rustling around in my postpartum underwear.

The envelope file was unmarked. The box file said, on the spine, REAL ESTATE—CURRENT CLIENTS—FOR FILING.

I stared at the box. Real estate. Current Clients. Crimpson. I thought for a moment or two. Hmmm.

Then I put it down, flushed and guilty. What was I thinking, for God's sake? I've been through this, I've thought about it and reached a moral conclusion, I apostrophized myself in a serious, philosophy-teacher kind of a way. It would be both professionally unethical and a serious wifely betrayal to look through Tom's private files.

Ethics Schmethics, another voice answered, a bolshy riot grrrl with her hands planted firmly on her hips. Is it ethical to leave your pregnant wife at home all day and to wantonly put your career above your kid? Riot grrls kick philosophy teachers' asses. I reached out my hands and picked up the box file, then lifted the lid and peered inside.

My fingertips seemed suddenly charged with electricity; my face was burning with a thrilling sense of terrible guilt. But the adrenaline quickly subsided: there was nothing in here to interest me. Just the usual lawyer's papers, court documents and case notes, shuffled together, some fastened together with large bulldog clips, others loose, in need of careful sorting. In fact, that must be why Leanne wants them, I thought to myself. She's set aside the morning to go through Tom's chaotic notes. Mentally I chastised my husband. Really, I thought virtuously, you need a better filing system. You have notes from about fifteen different clients, you'll never be able to find what you need—what's this, Fred Trask corporations, Billman & Hasselhoff Hotels, Gold-view Morgan Investments, Randalls's Developments...

Randalls's Developments. I swallowed. I had the oddest sensation of a thousand tiny red ants embedded in the skin of my palms.

I saw a bundle of notes, with a yellow Post-it on top, marked "Randalls's Developments" in Tom's crabbed, angular handwriting. About fifteen pages were clipped together—what are they, ah, a lease (was I relieved or not?) for a property uptown, on 128th—nothing about the building opposite, nothing at all to do with that. But wait—

Between pages seven and eight a letter, folded tightly in two, was slipped inside. I took it out. I opened it. I saw part of a sentence that read **"losing thousands in maintenance and taxes alone, that's before you factor in the potential market-rate rental income—"**

Hastily I shut the letter. What was I doing? My heart seemed to be attempting to leap out of my chest. I wondered what the baby was making of this scalp-crisping adrenaline surge. I thought for a moment or two. Something about Randalls's income, about its losses in a strong property market—it could be about anything, it's not necessarily about **my** building (as I seem to think of it now). In fact, it's probably about the lease to the

building on 128th. Yes, that makes sense. Reso-
lutely I slipped the letter back into the black box
file, then put both files on a chair near the door,
and heaved myself across the room to the sofa.

I lay down again, pulled the wool blanket over
my legs, and switched on the television. Judge
Judy was laying down the law, the real law that
is, the law of the people, not the fiddly stuff practiced by those of us in the trade. Judge Judy can't
do much to repair the damage wreaked by your
husband's lover to your family, your car, and your
self-esteem, but she can rain down moral invec-
tive for five minutes. She can truck in words like
right and **wrong** to make you, and all of us, feel
more secure. The gavel bangs. There! Resolution
without any of the tricky stuff, the who-pays-
what-when and which days of the week do you
see the kids, and who goes where for Christmases
and New Years and birthdays.

Don't stare at the black box file, don't stare at
the black box file, I said to myself, but I appeared
to be staring at the black box file. In fact, it seemed
to have taken an unearthly hold of my consciousness. I could almost swear it was **glowing** on
the chair by the door. "**Potential market-rate
rental income,**" a bland enough phrase, "**losing
thousands in maintenance and taxes**"—the
letter could be about anything, I reminded myself
again. The courier will be here any minute, and
I'll spend the day thinking it was about Mrs. G's

friends' building, and it probably isn't at all. Maybe—I thought to myself, at about 7:57 A.M.—the
best thing I can do is read the letter now, discover
it's about some matter entirely unrelated to the
building opposite, and then I'll forget all about it.
Yes, that's the best plan.

I threw off the blanket, stumbled over to the
chair, opened the file, rifled the pages, and took
out the letter.

CONFIDENTIAL MEMO it said at the top,
and it was written by Tom himself. In fact it was
a printout of an e-mail to Phil, his senior partner,
drafted four days ago. And this (as far as I recall)
is the substance of the document:

> **Phil—Things are out in the open
> with Valerie now, so you'll be on firm
> ground. I think Coleman Randall
> (the father) talked to her himself last
> week. He's arranged a meeting with
> John for Tuesday, but that's apparent-
> ly about litigating the shopping mall
> case (although knowing J. the issue of
> false submissions to the DHCR will
> almost certainly come up).**
>
> **I recommend you take Stewart
> along, he's up to speed on the back-
> ground. To summarize: Randalls
> were hemorrhaging money on the
> rent-controlled units at East Eighty-**

third—they were losing thousands in maintenance and taxes alone, that's before you factor in the potential market-rate rental income. Let's be clear: CR knew the DHCR has been hostile to applications to tear down properties in the last few years and he wanted the tenants out to give little incentive for further barracking. (He keeps referencing 823 Park in his defense without much understanding of the legal issues involved.) Stewart is certain he's outright lied about the state's position on both the scale of the mold and the procedures the state has enacted. He's only called us in because the tenants have got their hands on high-caliber legal counsel and he's terrified the whole thing is going south.

Clearly the tenants' lawyers will advise them to aim high, probably for punitive damages. This—and let's be frank here—is, after all, appalling behavior. I read CR the riot act about communicating with counsel and I broached the subject of correcting false submissions to the DHCR, which amount to—

And then the doorbell went. With hands that seemed suddenly stubbed and numb and fat, I refolded the letter and slipped it back inside the lease, but in which order—where did the lease go?—there's the doorbell again, shit, shit—I hastily shoved the bundle inside the black box file and snapped it shut, then opened the door, pinning my most charming and innocent smile to my face. The courier had the bored, bland expression of a man who risks his life every day on the West Side Highway. I gave him the files without meeting his eyes. He grunted at me incoherently, then disappeared into the stairwell.

And now I'm here in the apartment on my own—Mum's out hunting for a yoga class—and for the past hour I've been thinking to myself: what, precisely, have I found out, what do I know now that I didn't know before? The cogs of my brain seem to be turning with treacly slowness. First, that Randalls is on the run; the letter I told Fay to send seems to have worked, it sounds as if the tenants are about to start receiving the buyout offers to which they're entitled. But there's something else about the letter that interests me even more. Tom "read the riot act" to Coleman Randall. He advised him of his ethical obligations. He thinks Randall's behavior is "appalling."

This sounds like the man I thought I married. The Tom of the memo seems like a lawyer who thinks Alexis and Mrs. G have a point, that there's a battle to be won, and they're on the right side. And me too, of course. The only problem is, I shouldn't have read the file. I shouldn't know any of this, because I shouldn't have read the file. If Tom finds out I've looked through his confidential documents in order to find information to help my friends, he'll never trust me again. How have I ended up in the wrong here?

9:25 A.M.

Only one thing to do—

9:27 A.M.

I just called Tom. I picked up the phone and dialed the number with very little idea of what I was actually going to say to him. Beep, beep. "Hello?"

"Tom," I said urgently, and then stopped.

"Oh, it's you, Q," he replied, coolly. "What do you want?"

"I—er—just wanted to check that your files arrived. The courier came to pick them up at eight. They were on the table, by the kitchen," I babbled. "Beneath some of my stuff. Undies and things. Anyway I—ah—thought I'd check up on them," I finished, lamely.

"Yes, they're here, thanks," he replied, shortly.

There was a long, long silence.

"So—um—will you be home in time for dinner?" I offered at last, desperately.

"No, I won't be home," he said, flatly, "at least, I don't think I will. Look, Q, I'm incredibly busy right now, I'm under a deadline, I don't have the time to talk properly. I'll speak to you later, okay?" He put down the phone.

I've spent my entire adult life—hell, my life since I was thirteen—determined to have a strong, happy, successful marriage. I know what it's like to grow up in a house with an empty chair at the end of the dinner table. I know what it's like to absentmindedly set a place at that chair and then, with a sickening sense of horror and embarrassment, tidy it away again, hoping that no one else in the family has noticed. I know what it's like to catch a parent looking palely out the window with a look on her face that suggests, in an ideal world, she'd prefer to be swinging from a lamppost. I won't do that to a child of mine, I thought to myself as a teenager, digging my nails into the skin on the side of my hand, deep, deep, deep. The only thing my children will have to complain about is that their parents insist on kissing in front of them (**"eeuuuu, gross!"**). But as it turns out I seem to be handling this marriage about as badly as my parents before me—in different ways, and for different reasons, but just as badly.

65

My father was a short man, not much more than five feet eight. He had ginger hair (his legacy to me) and skin so pale that you could see the delicate blue veins in his wrists. I remember tracing them with my finger as a child, snuggled into the crook of his arm. He smelled of aftershave and Benson & Hedges.

When he left I cried every night for two weeks. I had my own room by then, so there was no reason to check my tears, no scared little sister to hear my sobs. I remember giving myself up to paroxysms of grief under the covers. How could he leave me with **her**? How was I going to live up to **her** standards? My father never had any standards for me, I suppose because he never had any for himself, and it made life a great deal easier. He was easily pleased with Bs. Hell, he barely noticed when I failed religious studies.

About three days after he'd gone I opened the laundry cupboard and found one of his shirts, yellow and brown checks, freshly washed, patiently awaiting its owner. I stared at that shirt for about twenty minutes. I actually sat down on the cork-tiled bathroom floor and gazed at it. I couldn't get my head around the fact that my father wasn't here and his shirt was. The following day I went back to the laundry cupboard, the secret shrine to my dad, only to discover that the shirt had silently vanished. But the wire coat hanger remained, bare, swinging backward and forward gently in the warm draft of air.

The first letter was incoherent. **Dear Q, I'm writing this to say I'm very sorry indeed and I miss you and Julie sends lots of love. I had to leave you know I did actually. I will come and see you very soon. Love Dad. xxxxxxxxx.** I put it into the pink velvet jewelery box given to me by my uncle one Christmas and now the repository of all my most treasured possessions. Contents: one charm bracelet, a free gift on the cover of some weekly girls' magazine; one silver thimble, a family "heirloom" according to my father; and every Christmas and birthday card my parents ever gave me.

These precious objects were soon joined by a second letter. **Dear Q, your daddy asked me to write and say hello. We are doing fine. I have eight guitar pupils now and he has joined a new band. It is going very well, although they recently lost their bass player and the saxophonist may be moving back to Belgium. We have just bought a dog called Cassie, you would love her. You must come down to Brighton and play with her. Your father says he'll phone or write soon. Love Julie. xx.**

I wasn't thrilled that Julie was writing his letters for him, but I dreamed about Cassie for months. Imagine what fun we'd have romping on Brighton beach! Cassie, in my mind, was a long-haired Afghan, or maybe a pure white sheepdog, and she was the very acme of fidelity—people who saw us together would be moved to tears by the deep and obvious bond between us. She would walk at my heel without a lead. She would save small children from drowning in response to my short expressive whistle. In the evenings I would comb her hair, and she would lick my hand and look lovingly up into my eyes.

My mother would never let us have a dog ("Too much mess, and I'm not coming home from work to walk the damn thing").

Needless to say, I never met Cassie. My father never invited me down. He rarely wrote to me, or to my sisters. Julie sent the odd card—uncomfortable, stilted, brief—and that was basically that. I used to wait in a state of anguished tension each December for their Christmas card, every year hoping to hear something new, to discover a change of heart on his part, something along the lines of: **Q, I'm sending this to you because you're the oldest and you'll understand. I had to leave because** [some terribly good reason followed here] **but I love you desperately and I really want to be a part of your life again. I can't stop thinking about you, imagining how you must have grown. I want to be a real father to you again.**

BED REST | 271

But each year I'd read something infinitely more anodyne. **Dear kids, Season's Greetings and a Happy New Year, lots of love, Dad and Julie. Hope you're all doing well. Band doing great, look out for the album!!!! xxxxxxxx.** As my teenage years passed I found myself fantasizing about bumping into him accidentally—say on a train; I'd see Cassie first, then I'd look up and see Julie (not that I was sure I'd recognize her, but I had a photo Dad sent us, which I retrieved from the bin my mother threw it into), and then at last—my father. He'd see me and his face would lighten—**Q, my God! I don't believe it!**—and he'd obviously be uncomfortable and embarrassed at first, but then—

The fantasy had two different conclusions. In the first, we'd get talking, and we'd soon discover we had all these points of contact. We liked the same kinds of music. We had a similar sense of humor. We both had flaming tempers ("to match the hair"). Julie would sit opposite us, watching us talk and talk, and she'd feel left out and nonplussed in the face of our renewed intimacy. By the end of the journey a whole new relationship would have kindled and we'd vow that nothing should part us again.

The second conclusion was rather different. My father would start talking to me, discover how adult I had become, and feel horrified at the thought of everything he'd missed, not to mention impressed with my new poise and maturity. He'd admit that I was the daughter he'd always felt closest to. Then he'd ask me to come down and stay with them in Brighton—he'd actually mean it this time—but I'd stand up and say something like, **you've got to be kidding! You think you can walk out on me, on all of us, and that I'm just going to forgive you? Don't you realize how much you hurt us? Dad, you are self-ish and immature. Mum has her faults, but at least she understood her responsibilities. She's been supporting us emotionally and fi-nancially all these years. You think I'm going to start a relationship with you now? No way! Forget it!** And everyone in the carriage would stare, impressed by my verbal skills and moved by my passion, then they'd turn to look disap-provingly at my father, and finally I'd walk away leaving him with his mouth hanging open, totally **crushed**.

But I never met him on a train. In fact, apart from a few brief awkward meals at McDonald's in the first year after he left, I never saw him again. One morning, at the end of my first term at uni-versity, I got a phone call. It was six o'clock, so before I even picked up the receiver I knew some-thing was seriously wrong. "Q, it's Mum here. I'm sorry to call you at this time, dear, but I've got terrible news." He'd had a heart attack—ap-parently he'd had lung cancer, not that we knew anything about it—and died in Julie's arms late the previous night.

So that was that; I never got the opportunity to play out either scenario with him. Julie wrote to me about a month after he died (she wrote to all three of us) to make a last rather desperate attempt to persuade us that our father really cared—"**He often talked of you, he was just too embarrassed to get in touch, he knew he'd let you down**"—and I wish she hadn't, it threw me for years. Should I have made the first move? Was it my fault we never saw each other? Was I in the wrong after all? But eventually I realized (to be perfectly honest, my therapist helped me realize) that **he** was the grown-up, **he** was the dad, **he** was the one who left. It wasn't my fault.

How does that Larkin poem go?

They fuck you up, your mum and dad.
They may not mean to, but they do.
They fill you with the faults they had
And add some extra, just for you.

The misery deepens like a coastal shelf...And so, Larkin advises sagely at the end, **Don't have any kids yourself**. Well, I'm about to break that rule. But how, how to stop the misery from deepening?

66

Tuesday 9 P.M.

I have another nonstress test, ultrasound, and fetal growth check scheduled for tomorrow morning. I think everything's going well in there, though; Mum has been filling me with good food all day, and the baby's been kicking crazily in response to the sugar. I doubt I'm going to get any sleep tonight, partly because of the small Scottish dancer in my stomach, partly because I can't stop thinking about the letter I read, illicitly, this morning.

Tom is definitely not coming home tonight. He called half an hour ago to say he's got to work straight through to tomorrow. I asked if there was anything I could do for him, if I could order dinner to be delivered to his desk, and there was a long, surprised pause. "I can do that for myself, thanks Q," he said finally, cool and reserved. "Just go to bed. I'll see you when I get home tomorrow evening. We need to talk."

I swallowed hard. Four words that fill a wife with horror: "We need to talk." I fear, I fear I know what that means.

67

Wednesday Midday

Where's a paper bag when you need one? I'm in the hospital again, on the edge of a panic attack.

The fluid seems to have gone. Poof! All gone. Vanished. Who knows where. I'm bewildered. "Did you have a leak?" Dr. Weinberg asked me; it made me sound like a frozen pipe.

I'm hooked up to a monitor, it's bleeping at me, numbers chasing one another up and down. 135, 142, 127, 132. Here we are again. So familiar.

Where is Tom? He's coming, he's on his way, he told me, a touch of hysteria in his voice, in my voice, when I called him from the ambulance on the way to the hospital. **Come quickly, they're going to cut me open in a few hours. They'll wait for you, not much longer. Please hurry. I** need **you.**

An hour ago, in the darkness of the sonography room, Cherise slid her probe across the convex arc of my taut stretched tummy through the usual dollop of blue gunge. This way, that way. Searching for black pockets. I stare at a screen above my head; I can see the long column of vertebrae, a tiny dinosaur curved around my belly button. No black here; a tiny patch here, something here, but there's a hand in the middle, it doesn't count, she tells me. I have to call Weinberg.

The doctor bustles in, businesslike, then slides onto the stool, picks up the probe, and stares intently at the screen. She mutters to herself ("one point two, one point three, nothing here, wait— no; one point zero here"); she pauses, starts again, sliding the probe deep down into my pelvis, pushing hard against the baby's shape. He moves away, indignant; my stomach undulates as he turns his shoulder on her. She smiles wryly.

My mother, sitting beside me, holds my hand tight, tight. "How big is he?"

Dr. Weinberg hits some buttons, wrinkles her forehead. "About six pounds, two ounces, I think," she says, with a shrug. "Hard to say."

I turn to smile at my mother, relieved. That's not a bad birth weight, I tell her, and he has nearly a week of growing to do still! My cesarean is booked for Monday.

Do Dr. Weinberg and my mother exchange a look?

A few more minutes of hard pushing, and Dr. Weinberg quietly, deliberately lays down the probe. She turns to face me; her face is oddly lit by the gray light of the screen. Her nose seems extraordinarily long, her cheeks high and angular. "It's time to call it quits, **bubeleh,**" she tells me, tenderly. "I want you to go straight into the hospital and have this child. Your pregnancy is over."

And air seems to be rushing too quickly into my lungs, and I'm shaking—"**Over?**" I gasp; "It can't be, I'm not due for surgery for another five days, and he might turn on his own by then, I've been doing my pelvic tilts **religiously,**" I tell her. Because suddenly I realize I've been hoping against hope that he **would** turn, that I'd be able to give birth "normally," like other women, like women do in films, with lots of grunting and shouting and pushing, followed by a moment of triumph and accomplishment.

But she tells me that she doesn't think he can wait for five more days; he needs to come out now, he's in immediate danger of compressing the cord and depriving himself of oxygen. "I don't think it's going to happen in the next hour, I'm happy to leave you on a monitor until your husband arrives. But if there is a problem while you're waiting, it'll be an emergency C, you understand? Put on your coat, I'm calling an ambulance to get you to the delivery suite. You're having a baby today."

Lights flash, they hook me up to a monitor straightaway, a dash through traffic—

I'm in a wheelchair racing down beige corridors, blue floors rushing toward me, pink doors opening—"Weinberg called about this one, she's here for a cesarean"—a plastic bracelet clipped to my wrist—"Take off your clothes"—the slitted robe again, my ungainly figure spilling out the back, my skin has never seemed whiter, those purple marks more apparent, soon to be joined by another, a slash across my pelvis—

Please, Tom, please come quickly, I can't imagine doing this without you. Please come!

11 P.M.

My son, Samuel Quincy, lies beside me. A new page for a new life.

68

Thursday 1 P.M.

Last night I was allowed out of bed for the first time in eleven weeks.

After the anesthesia wore off, the nurses helped me get up, and I walked on my own to the bathroom. The pain in my stomach is intense—I feel like I used to imagine a magician's assistant must feel after being put in a sparkly box and sliced in two—but the knowledge that bed rest is over keeps me going. They gave me morphine at first, now they've switched to some nice little white pills that go down easy and numb the worst of the incision's pain.

My son is sleeping; he seems exhausted by the last few days, as am I. He has his father's nose—and mouth, and chin. His eyes are unreadably dark.

They pushed him out twenty minutes after Tom arrived at my bedside. I was already being prepped for surgery beneath a hot green light when he surged through the doors, dressed in a paper suit that made him look like a henchman from one of those Bond movies set in the bowels of the earth. "Thank God I'm here," he kept saying, again and again. My mother quietly withdrew.

As they cut, he sat holding my hand, staring deep into my eyes. "Does it hurt? How do you feel? Are you sick?—Here, somebody, she's sick! She needs medicine! Is that better?" he asked, tenderly. I could feel the surgeon pushing beneath my sternum on the baby's head.

"I have the legs, and I'm pulling him out—out—out—and—here he is!" the surgeon called at last, and then, an upward lilt in his voice, "a healthy little boy!"

A pause, a brief moment of silence, and then a cry to make a mother's heart dissolve.

The doctors from the neonatal intensive care unit assess him and then leave, pushing their trolley, their instruments, their incubator, to another delivery room, another woman, another baby. I watch them go. They are not needed here. Our son is handed to Tom, whose expression fractures. Samuel Quincy gazes at his father in some surprise.

The three of us sit and stare at one another for the twenty minutes it takes the surgeon to stitch and staple me back together again. Tom and I ponder his resemblance to his grandparents. The baby keeps his counsel.

There is no sign of damage, they tell us, although he is smaller than we had hoped, at five pounds, eight ounces. But he is healthy, and his cry is loud and determined. ("I'm telling you, you'll have fun with this one," Dr. Weinberg says with a grin when she comes to visit us a few hours after the birth. She strokes his forehead with a crooked finger, and we say polite and grateful things to her, but she seems out of place in our room somehow, a vestige of another world, another life, already an ocean away.)

We slept a little last night, the three of us in one room together, my husband and I with a new sense of intimacy. Samuel owes his being to our love; his tiny body reasserts its existence.

Then, this morning, while Samuel slept in my arms, Tom came and sat on the bed beside us. He took my hand and looked at me over our baby son's head. "Q, I need to tell you something," he whispered, his blue-green eyes fixed on mine.

And my intestines froze. "Tom, please, don't," I whispered back; "don't tell me today, if you're going to leave me, don't tell me today, of all days."

As I stroked our son's fine curly hair with my free hand, I felt a hot tear run a course along the side of my nose.

My husband squeezed my hand hard. "Christ, Q, it's not that, look at me please, okay? Look at me! I want to tell you about a conversation I was having with Phil, the senior partner, yesterday morning, when you called from the ambulance."

I sighed wearily. "Oh I see—he told you when you're going up for partner, I suppose. The time frame, the practicalities, all that stuff. You can tell me all about it another time, Tom, really. We'll talk it through when I get home."

"Q, listen to me," Tom said, slowly and deliberately, "that's not what happened. What he told me is this: they're not going to recommend me for partner. It's over, Q. I didn't make it. I'm not going to make partner at Crimpson."

In my arms, baby Samuel snuffled, then opened his tiny mouth in a cat's yawn. He sighed and settled deeper into my breast.

I stared at my sleeping son, then at my husband. I couldn't quite believe what I was hearing. "They're not recommending you? But you've been working so hard, you've been doing so well, it's unbelievable, Tom, surely—" I said, astonished.

"No," he said, wearily. "It's not. Maybe it's because of these last few months—I'll be honest, I've been pretty distracted because of everything to do with you and the baby—but maybe that had nothing to do with it. I don't think I ever lived down those disasters of last year, and I didn't help my case by being 'self-righteous' (Phil's words) about Randalls these past couple weeks. The firm just wants to draw a veil over what's been going on, protect the client, do whatever it takes. Whereas I—well. **You** know, right, Q? Because you wouldn't do it either. It's one of the things I love most about you" (aiming a warm kiss at my ear). "Those guys deserve to be exposed, and I refuse to stop that from happening. Anyway, truthfully I think I've been dead in the water a while now at work; Phil said—he was pretty clear about it—that they don't feel I'm Crimpson partner 'material.' So I need to start looking for another job. Your husband is all but unemployed, what do you think of that?" His eyes were bright with tears. But it came to me suddenly that he wasn't nearly as sad as I would've expected.

"Things have been so bad between us, honey, these past few months; I should explain, I guess. I sort of knew my chances were slipping away at Crimpson. I was going crazy trying to stay on top of things at work, to make my case look stronger. And when things started going wrong I couldn't cope—"

Gently I reached over Samuel's head and cupped Tom's face in one hand. "I failed, Q," he said, a throb in his voice, "but I think the person I really failed was **you**."

Maybe he didn't actually say that, maybe I sort of wish he'd said it, but still, I'm sure that's what he meant. Or something close to it, anyway. I felt a sudden rush of tenderness.

Time—if ever there was a time—for Q's confession.

"Tom"—very hesitantly—"I did something ba—ad." I chewed my lip. Samuel was lying between us, how awful could his reaction be? "Pretty bad, actually. Tom, I was giving the Randalls's residents some advice these last few months, I felt so terrible for them, and the other morning I—er—I looked in your big black box file," I said, all in a rush, "the one you accidentally left at home. I found a copy of the letter you wrote to Phil about Randalls and I—I read it." He gasped. "You did **what**?" he said—Samuel's little body shifted slightly. He repeated himself, in a whisper this time. "You did **what**?"

He sat staring at me, his mouth open in astonishment. I investigated the cards in my hand and pondered which one to play. There's the joker—I'm a silly girl, I did a bad thing, but give me a kiss, bad boy, and let's forget all about it. Then there's the queen. Imperious, cool. Don't try the ethical thing with **me,** my friend, you're on pretty shaky ground yourself.

In the end I hedged my bets. It seemed to work. "Madness, Q, madness, but I guess you were going off your head on your own all day, and that's my fault," he offered when I was done. "And to be frank"—a ghost of a smile on his lips—"I kind of thought you might have something to do with all those red-hot letters from Schuster that started dropping through the mail." I grinned back and, when he turned away to pick up a glass of water, released a deep sigh of relief. His sense of loyalty to Crimpson was clearly passing; he kept referring to his firm as "them," not "us," I noticed, in the quick, warm, low-voiced conversation that ensued.

We couldn't do any of the fierce kissing we wanted to do because our son was fast asleep between us, and so, when the moment for words had passed, we sat and stared at each other over his tiny body and held hands very, very tightly.

Tom's back at our place right now, fetching baby clothes, toiletries for me, and my mother—she slept there last night. She has been extraordinarily good since the baby was born, quiet, unobtrusive, full of grandmotherly pride. "He is beautiful, Q," she told me, when I put my son into her arms for the first time. "Just beautiful. You've done a tremendous job. Really, a tremendous job."

69

6 P.M.

A visit this afternoon from Brianna and Mark.

"He is very cute," Brianna said, peering into the bassinet, "um, right numbers of fingers and toes, all that stuff, yeah?"

Everyone seems vaguely astonished that he doesn't have two heads. Clearly they've all been prognosticating dire consequences of the oligo for the last three months.

Mark carefully picked up Samuel out of the bassinet, then lifted him over his shoulder with a father's easy assurance. "He's a great-looking kid," he said, turning to Tom with a smile. "I'm so pleased everything worked out okay for you." He punched Tom's shoulder in a manly way, kissed my cheek, then produced a bottle of Piper-Heidsieck. We drank lukewarm champagne out of paper cups with graham crackers from the hospitality station in the corridor.

"So what do you think, guys?" Mark asked, with a hint of a smile. "Was it worth it, all that bed resting?" Tom and I looked at each other, then at Samuel, lying in Mark's arms. Was it worth it? Of course—"Although (and Q, I never said this to you, I thought it might knock your confidence) I'm not **convinced** it was necessary," Tom said, seriously. "Seems to me that when things go wrong in a pregnancy, and they don't know what to do, they send the woman to bed. All a bit Victorian, if you ask me. Still, you have to do what you can for your kids, right?" He smiled down at Samuel, who gamely threw his right arm in the air and biffed Mark on the chin. I nodded. You do what you can.

In the air, unsaid, was our shared knowledge of Lara's pregnancy. Mark will be back here in five months to meet his own son, a child who will enter the world one parent down, so to speak. I know Tom was thinking the same thing, because when he took Samuel from Mark he gave our little boy a surreptitious kiss on the head and held him extra close.

As Mark, Tom, and I talked about the birth, about breast-feeding, about the curious mixture of elation and exhaustion that succeeds the arrival of a child, Brianna seemed uncomfortable. Eventually she lapsed into a distressed silence. I tried to talk to her about things she could discuss—work, friends—but her eyes kept turning wistfully to Mark's preoccupied face ("After Edward's birth Lara could barely stand for a week, it's appalling to see the woman you love in so much pain, but at least Ed was a placid kid, not like Lucy, who howled from the moment her head popped out"). I told Brianna we'd take her out for a meal soon to thank her for her friendship and support these last few months, but I'm not sure she even heard me. They left us after half an hour in two very separate worlds.

Fay was next. "Just in between clients, shouldn't be here really, but I wanted to give you **this**"—this being a ridiculously enormous bouquet of hothouse flowers tied with a blue satin ribbon—"from the office. And to tell you we're looking forward to having you back, of course."

Of course.

"And to say that Randalls are folding like a pack of fucking—ah, Tom!"—as Tom arrived back with a fresh pitcher of ice water—"ahem, well, Q, you'll hear it all from your friends, no doubt, but I think you're going to approve of how that little matter has resolved itself. Incidentally when you get back to work we should talk about your pro bono cases, I'm willing to make space for you to take on more in the future. But look, I must get back, I have to file these goddam papers—where the hell's my briefcase—"

And off she went, into her own busy, lonely little world.

Ten minutes later, while I was in the middle of trying to force my left nipple into Samuel's resisting mouth, Mrs. G and Alexis appeared. Mrs. G watched the two of us fighting ineffectually for a few moments, then walked over, squeezed my nipple into a bullet shape, and rubbed it along Samuel's upper lip. He opened his mouth like a tiny baby bird and clamped down hard; a few seconds later I heard a swallowing sound. Once upon a time I might have found someone's grabbing my nipple a touch intrusive, but today, after sixteen hours of struggling to feed my child myself, I felt only gratitude. Alexis stared with the appearance of great interest at something out the window while my son nourished himself.

Mrs. G settled down onto the plastic chair beside me and produced a box of chocolates and a paper plate of Greek spoon sweets. Then, when Samuel slipped off my breast into a milky coma, she enfolded me in an enormous hug and told me her friends in the building opposite are saved—or, at least, that Randalls has begun to make some exorbitant buyout offers. Some of the tenants, she tells me, are likely to accept immediately, in order to put the whole experience at an end; others are talking about fighting to get more. But whatever happens, and whether the building is ultimately demolished or not, the rent-regulated tenants are going to get enough money out of this to find good accommodations for the rest of their lives. "And I know I have to thank you," Mrs. G said solemnly. "You do this. You sweet girl. You know, they make me good offer too, they want my place, and I think I'm gonna take it, move to the country, you know? I'm pretty tired of all this. Buy myself nice place, cook, enjoy my days. I miss **you**, though!"

And I'm going to miss her. She's my best—
only—friend in the neighborhood. We hugged
each other again, and she dropped a kiss on Samuel's cheek as she left. Alexis smiled vaguely at
me as he backed out the door; I watched him
go with a feeling of some regret. I quite enjoyed
ogling him these last few weeks, and I don't suppose I'll see much of him once Mrs. G's gone.
He'll be one of those people you smile at cheerily
on the street, until one day you don't anymore.
Mind you, I thought to myself, as my husband
uncrossed his legs and rose with a smile from his
perch on the hospital windowsill, now that's what
I call a bulge...

Lara came an hour later, Edward and Lucy
in tow. She looked wan, her cheeks hollow. "He's
a beautiful baby, Q, I'm so pleased everything
worked out okay," she said. "Your mother has
been fantastic, she brought me dinner these last
two nights, which is totally amazing, given that
she has a new grandson, and she even offered to
help me with the shopping. You're lucky to have
someone like that, you know. **My** mother barely
notices my existence, never did. Lucy, stop pulling Edward's pants down—for Chrissakes, stop
it! Have you guys seen Mark? No, I shouldn't ask
that, I'm sorry—LUCY! I've told you once already! He called me last night to say that he and
the girl plan to get married as soon as our divorce
is through. Hard to hear your husband talking

about marrying someone else. I'm sorry, Tom, I probably shouldn't criticize your friend, but I don't know if I can bear—LUCY! STOP IT! I should go, they're getting hungry again, and it's been a hard couple of weeks for them. I'll come and see you when you get home, that is if you don't mind, maybe you'd rather just see Mark in the future—?"

Tom and I both hastily assured her that we would stay friends with her, although truthfully I wonder if we will. It's hard to be friends with the spouse you were less close to when a couple separates. But still, remembering my mother's words, I told her if she needed someone to be with her during labor I'd be happy to partner her. She thanked me, although I'm not sure she really heard what I said because Lucy had finally managed to get Edward's pants down and was trying to stuff ice cubes into the legs.

Jeanie and Alison have both called in the last few hours to say congratulations. Jeanie put Dave on the phone for a few moments, and we exchanged grudging civilities; Alison put Serena and Geoffrey on the line and—well, I did my best to be nice to them. You have a new cousin, I told them, and he's going to enjoy playing with you very much. You're all going to be very, very good friends.

My mother spent much of the day here, although she periodically beetled off to do odds and ends of shopping. ("You'll want to come back to a well-stocked fridge, Q, and I'm hoping to get some meals in the freezer for you for after I've gone. I know I'm not a brilliant cook, but you'll be pleased to have a few spare veggie cobblers, won't you?") She did cause a mild fracas at one point by accusing a nurse of mishandling Samuel—"I'm sorry, dear, but she wasn't supporting his head properly, what would you have me do? Sit still and watch my grandson's neck get broken?"—but apart from that she has behaved in an exemplary fashion. It can't last, of course.

Peter and Lucille phoned a few hours ago to say they're on their way up from Baltimore to see us later this evening—"Peter has a tremendous amount of work this week, really, you've no idea, but he's going to make time to come up and see the—what is this, let me think, ah yes, his fourth grandchild," Lucille told me, blandly (lest I should flatter myself that I'm a bigger fixture in Peter's mental landscape than I really am). "But we knew you'd be **desperately** disappointed if we couldn't make it to see you and the little one, so we're pulling out all the stops—" Tom took over the phone just as I was starting to choke. "Really, Mom, it's fine, we won't be offended if—no, but Mom, you see—really—yes, okay, okay. Yes. We'll see you at nine, then. Great." He put down the phone with such a chagrined expression, I laughed. Lightly, happily. Peter and Lucille—bring them on. I can deal with them. Tom will have to tell them about Crimpson, he'll have to explain he's not making partner—but not today. We've agreed, it won't be today. Maybe we'll go a very long, long way away first (one of the Poles, perhaps), and then we'll call them.

Tom and I sit here and stare at Samuel, then at each other, and we look into the future. I don't know where we will go from here. We haven't talked about the kind of job he wants next, and we haven't begun to discuss my career. Where will we be a year from now? Will we still be living in Manhattan, raising our son while juggling two crazy professions? Or will we finally move to the 'burbs and turn our fantasy of Viking stove–ownership into reality? Or will we take a huge cut in pay, go somewhere totally new, and cultivate a slower way of life and perhaps a small vegetable garden? I don't know. But for the first time in months, when I look ahead, I see the three of us living together, and I like what I see. I'm putting a new item on the Modern Woman's List of Things to Do Before Hitting Thirty. Don't get too hung up on getting the boxes checked. Let the future take care of itself. (☑)

I listen to my son breathe. In, out. In, out. His chest rises and falls. I trace the tiny veins in his wrists that carry blood through his body, to his lungs, to his heart. I watch his eyelids flicker, his nostrils twitch. I nuzzle his ears, an incomprehensibly delicate arrangement of skin and cartilage. I pull his curled-up body, light and warm and wrinkly pink, into my arms, where he fits perfectly, like a cup in a saucer. And I think to myself—**I** created him! I did it!

About the Author

Sarah Bilston, originally from England, is married to an American and teaches at Trinity College in Hartford. **Bed Rest** is her first novel, and she is at work on the sequel, **Sleepless Nights**. She lives in Connecticut.

www.BedRestDiary.com
www.SarahBilston.com

Visit www.AuthorTracker.com for exclusive information on your favorite HarperCollins author.